Dear Robyn

Rainbow of Destiny

C.H. Admirand

Enjoy

_C.H._

C.H. Admirand

Published in the USA

C.H. Admirand
New Jersey
ISBN-13: 978-1540705693
ISBN-10: 1540705692

Cover Design by C.H. Admirand

Cover Photo: Killarney rainbow reflection
by Gabriel11/Depositphotos

C.H. Admirand

Books by C.H. Admirand

Historical Irish Western Series
The Marshal's Destiny
The Rancher's Heart
Pearl's Redemption
A Gift From Home
For Love of Flynn

Mo Ghrá Mo Chroí Go Deo Medieval Series
The Lord of Merewood Keep
The Saxon Bride
A Scot's Honor

Regency-Era Historical Trilogy
The Three Vices: Patience
The Three Vices: Charity*
The Three Vices: Prudence*

Contemporary Small Town Trilogy
A Wedding in Apple Grove
One Day in Apple Grove
Welcome Back to Apple Grove

Contemporary Western Romance Trilogy
Tyler
Dylan
Jesse

Contemporary Romance
Sullivan's Choice

*coming soon

Novellas and Short Stories by C.H. Admirand

Rainbow of Destiny
The Lady and The Rake
So Others May Live
Fear Not the Tarot: Temperance
Second Chance Ranch
Romantic Times: Vegas, Vol 2: Love at the Las Vegas Bake-Off
For Love of Flynn
The Seduction
The Duke, The Kiss, and The Vow
Legend of Love
Tall Dark Stranger
Champagne Kisses

Dedication

Family…it's the glue.

C.H. Admirand

Chapter 1

Bridget O'Halloran sat on the mossy bank of Killarney Lake, staring through the rain. Ignoring the chill settling into her bones, she waited, her gaze fixed on the water. The rain slowed to a fine misty drizzle and any moment now…

"Merciful heavens," she whispered. She blinked, but the vision remained. " 'Tis back." A tear slid across her cheek and down her neck. She wanted to jump up and spin about dancing with joy, but she did that last time and the vision disappeared. In her heart, Bridget knew she couldn't afford to throw away another chance.

Kneeling, she closed her eyes and concentrated. "Wish your wish," she told herself.

The last time the miracle happened, she had taken so long wishing her wish, the magic rainbow had vanished before she could speak. Determination gave her added courage. Even as she whispered the last of her wish, she looked up to make certain the rainbow was still there.

Her chest tightened with awe while a lump of emotion clogged her throat. As she reached out to touch the magic, her fingertips skimmed through the gray-green water, rippling the color. The mystic magic of the rainbow radiated warmth that seeped into her bones. She stirred the water again, captivated by the swirl of color that seemed to continue all the way to the bottom of the lake.

"Bridget O'Halloran," a breeze whisked past her cheek.

"Wh…what was that?"

The breeze swirled past her cheek again, but this time she felt a teasing touch along the line of her jaw and the soft fluttering of tiny wings.

Faerie wings.

Making a swift sign of the cross, she whispered, "Heavenly Father above, 'tis them."

She looked around her, straining to see, but her eyes refused to focus. Poised on the cusp of desperately wanting to believe that she wasn't imagining them, she prayed with all her might for a miracle.

A distinct rustling off to the left had her turning in time to see a blur of movement.

"I guess faeries don't really exist."

She drew in a deep breath, sighed, and turned back around. The lake and the shimmering rainbow formed the perfect backdrop for the dozens of winged faeries hovering in front of her. Clothed in blossoms and snippets of leaves, they were bright and bold as a bed of pansies.

One faerie slowly approached, and Bridget held her breath. When they were nose to nose, the fey creature smiled a slow impish smile. From the top of her ebony head to the tips of her bisque-colored toes, the tiny creature glowed. Bridget shook her head, not certain if her mind was wide-awake or asleep and dreaming.

"Who are you?" she asked the fey being.

"Alainn Ceo."

"Oh," breathed Bridget. "Beautiful Mist."

"Aye," *Alainn Ceo* replied with a toss of her ebony mane. " 'Tis in your favor that you speak the Irish, Bridget O'Halloran." The faerie paused, adding, "And 'tis about time you made up your mind."

The exquisite tiny being looked over her shoulder at the group hovering right behind her. They nodded in unison.

A deep voice rumbled up off the surface of the lake, calling Bridget's name, beckoning her to come forward. Fear skittered up her spine, and she shook her head.

"Any lass worth her salt would face what she wished for," the faerie challenged as her eyes narrowed to slivers of emerald. "Need I remind you to have taken care what you wished for, mortal?"

That brought Bridget back to her senses and to her feet. "I know exactly what I wished for," she said. "I wished for a man to love. One that would be strong and wise and love me forever."

Pausing, Bridget sighed. "In return, I promised to take care of him, give him bonny babes, and love him always."

The air crackled between her and the lake. The timbre of the voice, warm and deep, mesmerized her, drawing her toward it. Her curiosity got the better of her. She took the last few steps, dropped to her knees, and leaned over the lake. "Where are you?" she asked. "Show yourself."

"Open your mind and see with your heart. I am here." The deep voice wrapped itself about her, its vibration shaking her to the core.

"Well now," she said, "I'll try." She leaned farther forward, precariously balancing on the rim of the lake.

"Aye," the voice beckoned. "That's it, lass. Closer."

The beauty of the rainbow and the voice pulled at her. She inched forward just a bit more and caught a glimpse of a handsome face framed with black curls. He smiled up at her, his deep blue gaze holding her captive.

Her hand slipped, and she plunged over the edge. "Help! Hel—" Bridget's voice was smothered by the water of the lake as it closed over her head.

***

Duncan Garvey slowed to a crawl to take a long look around him. Some inner urge had him driving out to the lake today. He'd almost turned around, when the sun broke through the clouds, sending golden shafts of light spearing down from the heavens. He parked his car, got out, and stared at the rippling body of water.

Though he'd been to Ireland before, the rain-washed purity touched him deeply. He could almost believe the stories about the magic of the land. The lake lay like a jewel before him. Everywhere he looked, varying hues and shades of emerald abounded, from the verdant hills that rolled into fields of green, to the lofty trees. The beauty of the land grabbed him by the throat and held fast.

Though it was just after noon, he'd already put in a full day at his cousin's pub. He breathed deeply, staring out over the lake.

A gut-wrenching scream broke through the beauty and silence. He raced toward the sound and reached the edge of the lake in time to watch a woman go under.

He didn't stop to think. Years of training and instinct kicked in as he dove into the water. The shock of the cold made his head ache and his lungs burn, but he ignored it. Eyes open, he dove deeper, following the faint white of her lacy sweater. Reaching, he latched on to it and yanked her closer.

The weight of his clothes and boots threatened to drag him down, and for a heartbeat he couldn't move. Then a deep voice echoed through him, *"Don't give up, lad!"* He struggled to pull the woman toward the light, breaking through the surface of the water with one powerful stroke. He gasped, breathing deeply, struggling to pull air into his aching lungs.

One look at the pale woman, and he knew time was running out. Her face had a bluish tinge to it. *Not good. Definitely not good.*

He dragged the waterlogged woman up on to the bank beside him. Turning her onto her stomach, he began to force the lake water up and out of her. She coughed, and it was music to his ears.

What if he hadn't finished unloading kegs for his cousin ahead of schedule?

What if he'd stayed in town and not driven out to the lake today?

Smoothing the dripping strands of auburn hair off her forehead, he traced the line of her cheek. It was rose-petal soft. His water nymph was a beauty. Even as he thought it, her lashes fluttered open, revealing slightly dazed whiskey-colored eyes.

Though his heart still raced from the affects of the cold water, and fear that he wouldn't reach her in time, he dug deep for a calm he didn't feel. Keeping his voice low, hoping to sound encouraging, he asked, "Who are you?"

She drew in a breath to speak and burst into a spasm of coughing.

The dregs of fear combined with temper, and he bit out, "What in God's name were you doing swimming this time of year?" He glared down at the beautiful, wet woman. She'd stopped coughing and stared at him.

He swore under his breath. "Are you crazy?" Not waiting for an answer, he swept the helpless woman up in his arms and settled her against his heart. Her womanly curves distracted him and he stumbled on a loose rock, as his weak leg gave out.

"Damn." The injury was still too new to be strong, but he ignored the pain putting her safety first.

The woman in his arms made a soft sound, and he forgot about the pain and looked down.

"Alainn Ceo," she whispered.

"Alainn?"

She shook her head, and little droplets of icy lake water splashed in his face. "She's gone."

Worry lanced through him. Had she been in the water too long without air? Had her mind snapped? "But you're right here."

She shook her head a second time. "I'm not *Alainn*."

"Then who is?" he asked.

"A faerie."

Chapter 2

She smiled at him. "You were worth the waitin'."

He raised his eyebrows at her odd statement. "Did you hit your head?" He opened the passenger door and slid her onto the seat.

"No. Why?"

He shut her door, stalked over to his side, and yanked the driver's door open. *Why him?*

"The faerie," he grumbled, slamming the car door and jamming the keys into the ignition.

"Well, aren't you goin' to ask me?" Her voice sounded hoarse. "Not that I could say yes until I be knowin' your name." She wrapped her arms about herself.

Was she trying to hug some warmth back into her chilled body? Of course she'd be cold; she was in the water longer than he was.

Which one turns on the heat? As he fumbled with a few switches on the unfamiliar dashboard, he couldn't keep from asking, "Say yes to what?"

Bridget tilted her head to one side and watched him, waiting.

Heck, he couldn't read minds. "I'm cold and wet and don't have all day." As soon as the words were out of his mouth, he regretted his harsh, angry tone.

He didn't want her to be afraid of him, and from the uneasy look on her face, knew she was. He blurted out, "I'm sorry."

She shrugged and glanced out of the window.

"Won't you tell me your name?"

She turned from the window, holding his gaze for a few moments before finally answering, "Bridget O'Halloran. I live just over the hill there." As she pointed, her arm gave away the fact that she was shaking.

Duncan swore under his breath. She needed heat fast! Finally finding the switch for the heat, he cranked it up to high. Following in the direction she'd pointed, he turned onto a narrow lane that led right up to the bright yellow door of a quaint thatched cottage.

"Is anyone else home?" *Please let there be someone. I've got to get back to the pub and some sanity.* He got out of the car and walked around to help her out. She looked so fragile he didn't ask if she could walk. He made the decision for her, sweeping her into his arms and kicking the car door shut.

"I live alone," she rasped as he shifted her in his arms and tried the door. Finding it unlocked, he opened it and carried her inside.

"Do you have any neighbors you could call to come and sit with you?"

"You cannot be leavin'," she whispered. "We've just met and I haven't—"

"Look, I'm sorry." Duncan worried about the panicked expression marring her lovely face. "But I have to get back in time for the five o'clock delivery."

Settling her on the sofa, he reached for the blanket draped across the back of it, and wrapped it around her. His gaze met hers and he felt the bottom drop out of his stomach. Tears glistened in her whiskey-colored eyes

He could face blood, death, and destruction, and had on a daily basis before quitting the force. But tears unmanned him. He groaned as she blinked and they spilled over.

Knowing he couldn't leave yet, he asked, "Can I use your phone?"

"Don't you have a cellular one?" she asked, pulling the edges of the blanket he'd draped about her closer.

"It was in my back pocket when I dove into the lake."

Her eyes widened as realization dawned. "Oh. Sorry." She gestured toward the back of her cottage. "The phone's in the kitchen."

As he stepped into the kitchen, she called out, "But you don't need to summon help on my account."

Exasperated, he shook his head. "I want to tell my cousin that something's come up, and I'll be late getting back."

"Oh."

That one word was packed with hidden meaning, if the look on Bridget's face was anything close to what she was feeling.

"I'll just be a minute." He called the pub and briefly explained what happened, wanting to end the call quickly because a loud chattering was coming from the sofa.

"Do you have any matches?" he asked, walking toward her.

She sniffed and grumbled, "I can light a fire if I want to."

He looked over his shoulder at her, and waited, sensing she wasn't finished speaking.

She wasn't. "I don't need a fire."

"I suppose it's *Alainn's* teeth I hear chattering," he said. "Not yours."

Bridget flushed a becoming shade of pink. His gut clenched for the second time in the last hour. This time, it wasn't a reaction to fear. The heightened color accentuated her porcelain skin. Her beauty captivated him.

Needing distance, he walked toward the fireplace and noticed a box of stick matches lying on the mantelpiece. He knelt in front of the fireplace and went to work laying a fire. Once the kindling caught and burned brightly, he added a few logs.

Satisfied with the crackling heat pouring out of the fieldstone fireplace, he turned around in time to see Bridget trip on the blanket tangled around her legs as she tried to stand.

He caught her before she hit the floor and dread filled him. "You feel like a block of ice."

Tremors wracked Bridget's body, forcing him into action. "Where can I find dry towels and strong whiskey?"

"Kitchen cupboard," she whispered. "Left of the door."

She was shaking violently now, and the worry of hypothermia washed over him. Drawing on the calm he used daily when called to protect and serve; he followed her directions and pulled out two thick cream-colored towels. He turned, intending to ask about the whiskey, but she was already pointing toward the cupboard.

"The *Jameson's* on the top shelf next to the fridge." Pausing, she added, "Glasses are on the other side."

He found everything exactly where she'd said it would be. Although he'd never been an orderly person by nature, he appreciated the fact that she was. Duncan poured three fingers and handed her a short, heavy glass. "Drink up."

"I cannot drink with a man I've yet to be properly introduced to."

Surprised that her fragile looks didn't match her sharp tongue, he felt himself smile for the first time since he'd pulled her out of the lake. "I was wondering when you'd get around to asking me."

Her sweet smile seemed hesitant, waiting for him to speak.

"It's Duncan," he said. "Duncan Garvey."

She nodded, but didn't move.

"Drink up," he told her. "Then you can take off your clothes."

Her gasp cut through the stillness. "I'll do nothing of the sort, until we're wed."

He shook his head. "My intentions are strictly honorable, Miss O'Halloran."

When she still didn't do as he asked, he frowned and bit out, "You're in danger of hypothermia. The whiskey will do for a start warming you up on the inside, but the wet clothes have to go."

***

Comprehension dawned, and her belligerent look changed to one of concern. She tossed back the whiskey and shook her head at him when he reached for her. He ignored her unspoken hint that she didn't need his help and tugged at the edge of her blanket. She slapped his hand away.

His smile was slow and had the breath backing up in her lungs. Her world tilted just a bit off to the left. She knew that face; trusted that face; because he was the man she saw reflected in the lake…the one she wished for!

He reached for the blanket a second time, asking, "Are you sure you don't need my help?"

Teeth clenched to still the chatter, she bit out, "I do not." Taking a step back, he raised his hands high and turned around. "Okay."

Hands shaking, knees weak as water, she struggled to stay upright. Lord, she'd never been this tired. Her arms felt like lead weights were strapped to them, but worse, her legs refused to work. Holding on to the back of the chair she realized she was being stubborn.

Maybe he was right.

Bridget gripped the chair with one hand, determined to give it one last try. The wave of dizziness took her by surprise.

After a few failed attempts, she knew she'd have to swallow her pride and ask for help.

Duncan's sapphire gaze locked with hers. "You'll end up in the hospital if we don't get your body temperature back to normal." He pulled her sodden sweater off, ignoring the fact that she stood before him in her underwear and wrapped a towel around her.

Working quickly, he unzipped her skirt. It landed on the floor with a squishy plop.

The shock of his warm hands on her chilled skin befuddled her brain. He wrapped her in the other towel. His touch had her struggling to calm her racing heart.

Today was filled with firsts for her. No man had undressed her before, and she'd never trembled at a man's touch. Meeting his steady gaze, she wondered if he knew his touch affected her.

Bold blue eyes, dark and unsettling stared at her. Maybe it was the dunking in the lake and nearly drowning that muddled her thoughts, or maybe it was destiny, but she met his gaze and smiled.

"Your turn." But before she could help unbutton his shirt, he gently brushed hers aside. "Go and sit in front of the fire," he urged, "I can manage."

Self-preservation had her stumbling to the sofa and curling up like a cat, feeling the warmth of the flames heating her face. She sighed wondering how long it would take for the rest of her to thaw out when she heard the hiss of a zipper, followed by the wet thud of his jeans hitting the floor.

Unable to resist a peek, she glanced over her shoulder in time to see he'd wrapped a towel around his waist and was drying his hair with another.

Her brain simply shut off, distracted by the sheer beauty of his face and form.

***

Perched on the sofa, draped in towels, her beauty beguiled him. An errant copper-colored curl caught on her eyelash and held fast. He loosened it and brushed it off her smooth forehead.

Her smile bloomed like one of his mother's roses, shy and hesitant at first, then boldly blooming adding color to her cheeks and a sparkle to her eyes. Everything she felt reflected in her gaze.

He was man enough to admit to he liked that her eyes all but popped out of her head when he stood before shirtless. But her reaction paled in comparison to the moment he held her in his arms and an emotion he couldn't name grabbed a hold of him and refused to let go. It was almost as if…

No, he thought, fate couldn't be that perverse. He'd left home and crossed an ocean to forget the one woman he'd trusted his heart to. He wasn't going to let another distract him, no matter how sweetly she smiled at him.

Taking a step back, he reached for the bottle he'd placed within reach. "You're still shivering. You need another shot of whiskey."

Though the longing in her eyes beguiled him, they'd only just met and he wasn't willing or ready to dive into another relationship based on looks alone. Remembering the faerie she thought she saw, he wasn't entirely certain she wasn't just this side of crazy. Oh, his mom had told him fantastic tales of faeries, leprechauns and the banshee, but he'd grown up and stopped believing in magic the first time he'd faced down a loaded gun in a dark alley. Training and speed were what he'd needed on the job...not luck or magic.

He poured another two fingers in her glass and was tempted to toss the hard lessons he'd learned in life right out the window. But sanity returned as he watched her sip from the glass, a beautiful woman and spontaneous physical attraction had been the basis for his last relationship. And that'd shattered, just like his leg, when she'd heard the news he'd been shot.

Bridget's wary but intense curiosity pulled at him. He watched her watching him. A dangerous move, because she tempted him to the point of pain as every cell in his body strained against his control. He fought with every ounce of grit he had.

She sighed but drank deeply. He waited for her to stop shivering, but a double dose of whiskey, dry towel, and spot in front of the fire still hadn't helped. Her slender frame still trembled.

His training was so ingrained he knew not to ask, because she might not be coherent enough to accept what he had to do. Duncan swept her into his arms and sat down, holding her against him until, the combined heat from his body and the fire warmed her, and the tremors gradually stopped. She let out a long deep sigh and drifted off to sleep.

Contentment filled him as he let himself relax against her. Exhaustion had him closing his eyes, just for a moment.

Chapter 3

"What's goin' on here, Bridget?"

The deep voice roused Duncan from a sound sleep. He opened his eyes to see a fist coming toward his nose.

Pain screamed through his face as the rest of him woke up in time to feel the second blow to his left eye.

Memories of stakeouts gone bad flashed through his aching head as he wondered what he had done. Where the heck was he?

"Dermot, you *eedjit*!"

The woman's voice sounded familiar.

"Stop!"

Duncan blearily focused on the fiery-haired vision draped in a towel, and his mind instantly cleared. "Bridget, what's going on?"

A ham-sized hand in the middle of his chest stopped him from reaching for her. "Who the hell are you, and what have you done to my sister?"

Duncan wasn't given a chance to explain. The hand fisted and pulled back a second before plowing into his solar-plexus.

Gasping for breath, he could only shake his head.

"Leave off, Dermot!" Bridget warned, shoving the hulk who claimed to be her brother aside.

"His name's Duncan Garvey," Bridget bit out. "He saved my life." She pressed one hand against her breast to keep the towel in place and used the other to help Duncan to his feet.

"Is everything all right, Dermot?"

Another man's voice had Duncan looking over his shoulder. The knuckle-dragger standing in the doorway to the cottage had the spit drying up in his mouth.

The guy reminded him of the coked-up, ex-pro football player he and his partner had taken down. Duncan thought Bridget's brother was big, but this guy dwarfed him.

"What have ye done to me bride?" the man demanded, stalking over to Duncan, fists raised, eyes black with rage.

Bridget shoved Duncan behind her and held out her hand. Duncan knew his next breath could be his last. "He's given me a gift beyond compare."

The huge man stopped in his tracks and looked from Duncan to Bridget and back. Duncan would later swear he saw steam coming out of the man's ears a heartbeat before pain exploded in his jaw and everything went black.

***

"Are you out of your mind?" Bridget demanded.

"You're the one whose wits have gone beggin'," the big man snarled. "Where are your clothes?"

"Where he left them after he took them off me," Bridget said.

"I'll kill him," the two men said simultaneously.

"No, you won't," Bridget stood her ground. "You've both heads of granite, and you're not listenin'."

"Just because he saved your life isn't reason enough to give him your innocence," the big man wailed.

Her eyes narrowed to slits of amber. "If I did, it would be my decision."

"But Bridget, we're promised—"

"I've not said I'd marry you, Sean."

"But—" her brother began.

"And you both know it," she interrupted, slanting a look over at her brother.

"But I keep hopin'," Sean rasped.

"And I keep tellin' you, I've dreamed of the man I'm fated to marry," she said quietly. "I'm sorry, Sean. You aren't the man I've seen." She waited a few moments for her words to sink in, and then asked, "Will you help me lift him onto the couch?"

When neither one made a move toward her, she put her hands on her hips and rasped, "Now would be a good time."

Her brother and his best friend lifted Duncan and laid him on the couch.

"Get me a damp rag," she asked. When they both hesitated, she added, "Please?"

"Can you at least put some clothes on?" her brother asked.

Looking down, Bridget was reminded she was wearing her underwear beneath a towel. "Um, yes." Straightening, she walked toward the stairs and nodded at her brother. "See that you get a damp rag and wipe the blood off Duncan's face while I'm gone."

Bridget tugged on an old flannel shirt and loose-fitting jeans. Rushing, she dashed downstairs and stopped in her tracks. Duncan was awake and trying to push Dermot and the cloth he held away.

"Duncan, wait," she called out.

His blue eyes locked with hers. "Why? So you can explain again how I've saved your life, and your brother and his overgrown friend can beat the crap out of me?"

"But you did save my life, Duncan," she whispered. "And I'll be forever grateful."

"You have a strange way of showing gratitude."

Duncan finally managed to push Dermot aside and struggle to his feet.

"I've yet to thank you properly," she said, walking toward him.

Duncan swiped the back of his hand under his nose and spread blood across his cheek and his hand. Looking at it, he shook his head. "Save it."

"But Duncan—"

The slamming of the door sounded so final. Her hopes plummeted, and her heart sank. The love of her life, the one the faeries and the magic rainbow conspired to reveal to her, saved her life but wanted no further part of it.

"He should have let me drown."

"Are you daft?" Her brother's question was a valid one. *Was she?* She hadn't hit her head that she remembered, but then again, she had swallowed at least a gallon of lake water.

"Surely, you don't wish that," Sean murmured, coming to stand beside her.

"How would you know?" she asked. "You've never once listened to a word I've said."

"I have—" he began.

"Not," she finished for him. "I've told you, a hundred times, the man I'll marry isn't from Ireland."

"But I thought you were just sayin' that," he whispered, staring at the tips of his shoes. "As your way of playin' hard to get."

"You're the one who's daft, Sean," she said, squeezing his hand in friendship. "You're a grand friend to Dermot and myself." Bridget hoped he'd believe her this time. "But I can't marry you...especially now."

"What happened?" Dermot asked, coming to stand beside them.

Bridget walked to the front door and urged Sean on his way. Then turned to say, "I've got to talk to Duncan, to explain."

"You aren't going anywhere until you tell me the whole of it." Dermot's voice had gone soft.

A bad sign, that.

Chapter 4

Michael Sweeney winced when he saw his cousin's battered face. "Well then…'tis true."

Duncan didn't want to talk about it, but he knew he'd have to, or be plagued with Michael bugging him for the rest of the day. Duncan sighed. "What's true?"

"Ye ran into the O'Halloran and Mulcahy."

Duncan waited for Michael to say more, but his cousin walked over to the stack of boxes in the back of the pub.

"I need ice." Duncan needed aspirin, too. A handful ought to be enough to cut through the vicious pain in his face and jaw.

"What I'm not understandin' is why you were even at O'Halloran's place and what you were doin'."

The anger he'd been keeping a lid on burst free. "Nothing," Duncan bit out. "I wasn't doing one darned thing."

"But you were both naked." Michael's eyes were alight with accusation and interest.

Duncan closed his eyes and breathed deeply. When he opened them a moment later, he felt back in control.

"No we weren't," he insisted.

"Nearly naked, then," Michael said.

"Wrapped in towels still wearing our underwear, damnit!"

His cousin's raised eyebrows had Duncan's temper simmering.

He walked to the kitchen and pulled out a tray of ice, emptying half of it into one of the linen bar towels he'd found stacked on the counter by sink. Was there ever any point in trying to talk sense into his hard-headed cousin?

"Nothing to tell." He knew Michael wouldn't let it lie for long, and he was right.

"But Mulcahy's goin' to marry Bridget."

Duncan couldn't say why the woman he'd fished out of the lake marrying the behemoth who punched him bothered him. "I wouldn't bet the farm on that, Mike."

He sighed the beautiful, water-drenched woman had the most kissable mouth.

He still couldn't get the idea out of his head. He'd resisted earlier, but now…now he wasn't so sure it had been a good idea. Her lips would be soft but firm and would've taste like heaven. "I've work."

His cousin stared at him. Duncan grabbed the ice-filled towel, and walked back out the way he'd come in.

The small yard behind the pub was empty. He'd nearly wished for the company of one of the cats who made Sweeney's Pub a nightly stop on their sweep of the neighborhood in search of free food. But it was too early in the day for that; he'd have to wait.

Sitting on the beat-up wooden bench by the corner of the building, he leaned against the sun-warmed stones. The cold seeped through the towel while he tried to decide where to put the ice first, then realized it didn't matter. His whole face hurt...nose, eye, and jaw.

All he'd been doing was trying to keep the woman from drowning and then from freezing. Hypothermia on top of nearly drowning, just the thought of it made him crazy.

He sighed deeply, why should he care anyway? She was a female, and all females were trouble. The disastrous outcome of the last drug bust that went bad had put him on permanent disability. Add to that his ex-fiancee's reaction to his disability, and after he'd finished with physical therapy, he'd high-tailed it out of Boston to work for his cousin Michael in the family pub in Ireland.

"Ahh," his cousin said from behind him. "There you are."

Damn. And here he thought he'd finally be alone. When he'd driven out to the lake earlier on his break, he thought he'd be able to relax at least for a little while and maybe sort through the reasons he'd run to Ireland. But he hadn't had time to think earlier, or get the break he desperately needed. Apparently, he wouldn't be geting one now.

"I know I promised not pry into your life while you were over here workin' for me and mine." Michael said, coming to a halt in front of Duncan. "You've had a rough time of it recuperating, then doing physical therapy and all. But I cannot understand why you took advantage of Bridget."

Duncan closed his eyes. Why should he defend himself when even his cousin didn't believe him?

"Kin or not, I ought to take you apart, boy-o," Michael warned.

Why were the Irish so thick-headed and stubborn? "All I did was save her life!"

"Then why did Dermot and Sean try to take you apart?"

"Just my lucky day," Duncan mumbled, shifting the ice onto his jawline. The throbbing eased just enough to be bearable.

Michael's sigh was loud and long. "If you'll tell me your side of the story, maybe I can understand better."

"And you'd believe me?"

His cousin sighed. "I'll try to but, can you not see this from my perspective?"

Duncan lifted the ice off his aching face and glared at his cousin. "And by that, I'm sure you mean that your unsullied reputation in town is worth more than Bridget's life, or mine, or the brand new boots and cell phone that were totally trashed when I dove into the damned lake!"

Michael's shrug irritated Duncan almost as much as his need to ask his cousin whether or not the lovely Bridget was going to marry the hulk of man named Sean.

He didn't know why he cared and couldn't figure out why it should bother him if she married the guy. He hadn't cared about much since the night he took a bullet in the leg and nearly lost it.

Michael gave him one last look and turned on his heel and walked away.

Duncan stared at his feet and wondered if the cold water had affected his brain, because all he could think about was a pair of lovely amber eyes and skin soft as a rose.

"Here." His cousin pushed a glass of water at him and handed him two pills.

Without looking, Duncan grunted and accepted the peace offering, tossing down the pills and draining the glass. Maybe they'd be able to talk about it later. He had a couple of questions for Michael Sweeney.

***

And I told you exactly what happened," Bridget huffed. "Can you not let it go?"

"No."

She glared at her brother and wished for the hundredth time that he wasn't so protective. She'd been living on her own for two months, and still he couldn't go one day without stopping by and checking up on her.

Irritating man.

"Well then," she said slowly, considering just what to do to get her brother out of her house and on his way down the road.

She opted to be brutally honest. "I've told you what happened, and you choose to believe that I'm lacking in brains and morals."

Her brother opened his mouth to speak, but she drilled her pointer finger into his chest and told him, "I'm not finished yet, boy-o."

His eyes rounded in shock, but he held his tongue.

Just when she was ready to tell him what she thought of him, she remembered the day she'd tossed that handful of dirt onto the top of their Da's casket and Dermot had wrapped his strong arm around her, holding her up until the last prayer had been said and the last of the mourners had gone home. Then her brother had held her while she cried her heart out.

The memory had her swallowing her anger and asking him to go home.

When he stared at her, she asked again, "Would you please, just go home? You'll be welcome back when you're ready to apologize for thinking ill of me and the man who dragged me out of the lake."

The rest of the words she'd wanted to say burned on her tongue, but words spoken in anger were usually the most hurtful. She swallowed them, gave his hand a quick squeeze, and pushed him toward the door. "Please?" she begged.

Dermot's face flushed crimson, and his eyes blazed with anger, but he nodded and walked past her out the door.

Bridget didn't realize she was shaking until she tried to latch the door unsuccessfully for the third time, but not from the cold…from anger.

Why couldn't Dermot and Sean believe her?

Exhausted and chilled to the bone, they'd simply fallen asleep. Yet her brother and his friend, the man who'd mistakenly thought she'd marry him simply because he'd asked tried to twist it around and make it into something it wasn't—something more than it had been, tainting the purity of the innocent act it had been.

Being held close to Duncan's heart, held safe within the warmth of his arms, had allowed Bridget to do something she hadn't done in months—sleep.

She was jolted by the realization that she hadn't woken until her brother and Sean barged in. Why had she felt so secure with Duncan?

Was it a fluke, or was it because he was the one she'd seen in the lake?

It didn't matter because she'd never see him again. She finally managed to latch the door. Walking toward the kitchen, she lit the burner and leaned against the kitchen table, waiting for the tea water to heat. Duncan Garvey had made it plain to all who happened to be listening that he wanted nothing to do with her and would not be seeking out her company again.

How then could she wed the man if he refused to see her?

A smile spread slowly across her drawn features as an idea took hold. She'd just have to seek him out. Maybe he was just playing hard to get. An American term Sean used to describe her avoiding him, the *eedjit*.

But your brother and blasted ex-beaux beat him senseless while he was still half asleep and unable to defend himself. Her mind insisted. *He's not likely to listen to you.*

"But maybe if I could just explain…"

The words drifted off into silence. If his parting words were any indication of the way he felt, Duncan wouldn't want to see her again.

But he was her hope, her future, her destiny.

Fortified with those thoughts, no longer needing the tea; Bridget turned off the whistling teapot and walked over to the staircase. As she ascended the steps, she wondered what one should wear to see one's future husband.

Chapter 5

An hour later, she walked into Sweeney's Pub and let her gaze sweep the room. Michael wasn't anywhere to be seen. His younger brother, Patrick was manning the bar. No sign of Duncan at all. *The coward!*

How could he let her brother and his ham-handed friend scare him into hiding? Maybe Duncan wasn't the man of her dreams. Maybe he was just a temporary man in her life until the true man of her dreams came along. She shook her head at that thought. Duncan was the one who had pulled her out of the lake at Killarney; her heart reminded her stubborn head. His face had been reflected in the water. Duncan *was* that man.

Remembering his parting words, her head insisted, *not bloody likely.*

Irritated by the turmoil raging inside of her, she braced herself and realized there was no time for soul-searching. The faeries and fate had revealed her future husband to her. He was the one...black-haired and blue-eyed. Something stirred deep inside of her when she remembered the warmth of the rainbow in the water and how his reflection had appeared in the depths of the lake.

Stubborn man.

As if her thoughts conjured him, he stood before her with his eye black, chin bruised, and lip split.

"Oh, Duncan," she rasped. "You must be in terrible pain." She walked to the back of the bar where the door to the kitchen stood half-opened, and her battered future husband stood swaying on his feet.

"What do you want?"

His bitter tone arrowed through her, but Bridget strove not to let it show. She'd become a master at hiding what she felt from her older brother and then from Sean, not letting anyone see the depth of her sorrow. But if the man's bruised face were any indication, he didn't believe the look of disinterest she feigned.

When she continued to stare at him, he threw his hands up in the air, spun on his heel, and stalked back into the kitchen.

"I thought you were goin' to help Patrick at the bar," Michael began, until he noticed Bridget standing in the doorway. "Well, now." A knowing grin spread across his freckled face. "I'll just leave you two alone."

He side-stepped the glaring Duncan and patted Bridget's shoulder as he swung through the door.

"Are you deaf?" Duncan finally asked her.

She looked at him. *What an unusual question.* He had to know she wasn't. She shook her head.

"Then perhaps you could answer my question before you leave."

She smiled at him, hoping the source of his anger was because his feelings for her were conflicting with his need for self-preservation. "Hmmm, what question?"

Poor man. His face looked so sore. "Have you put ice on that?"

He closed his eyes and tilted his head back.

When he didn't look at her right away, she worried that he'd injured his brain as well. "Are you sure you don't need medical attention?"

"And have half the town know that I couldn't handle a few punches from O'Halloran and Mulcahy?" He snorted.

The sound skittered up her spine, leaving her feeling bereft and cold. "I think that butterfly bandage over your eye is too loose," she warned, hoping she could talk him into going to the doctor with her. If not the doctor, then perhaps the hospital. The longer she looked at him, the more convinced she became that he needed medical attention rather desperately. The man swayed on his feet, and his eyes were struggling to stay open.

He closed his eyes again and swore. "What do you want?"

He rubbed at his temple, mumbling something about what his cousin gave him. He swayed, but before he could stumble, Bridget wrapped her arms around him. She led him over to the chair by the back door.

"Here now," she soothed, knowing she'd eventually have to answer Duncan's question. "Just a bit of an uneasy head. Rest now, and I'm sure we can summon the doctor to have a look at you."

"I don't want anyone else to look at me," he bit out.

Grumpy and battered, he still stopped her heart with his looks. Biting down on her lip, she realized she had it bad. She, Bridget O'Halloran, had finally been bitten by the bug, the love bug, and more's the pity, the man she loved couldn't care less.

"Nevertheless," she began as Duncan's eyes rolled up in his head. Fear tore through her. "Michael!"

More than one man came running when she screamed. Duncan barely stirred, while Michael lifted him up by one arm and Patrick supported him from the other side.

"He was talking, and he just keeled over." Bridget struggled not to burst into tears. The day had been trying enough with seeing the fey by the lake, finally having her wish granted, gazing upon the face of her future husband, and then nearly drowning.

But nothing hurt her heart or worried her like the sight of Duncan being half-carried out to Michael Sweeney's lorry. "Careful not to hit his head."

Michael glared behind her and nodded. She had a feeling she knew who stood behind her, and the thought was confirmed when a heavy hand came to rest upon her shoulder.

She sighed deeply. "I thought I told you to leave me be."

"And I thought I told you I promised Da I'd look out for you after he'd died."

Guilt-laced sorrow edged through the worry squeezing her heart. "I know you did, and most times I'm grateful."

"But not this time," Dermot finished her unspoken thought.

"I don't know why Megan McCourt thinks you've wits to let, Dermot." She tried to smile and almost managed it. "If you put your mind to it, you're a sharp one."

"She pines for me when I don't go 'round and see her at the flower shop."

Bridget found she could smile after all. "Nearly every breath she takes." It was an old game between them, lifting each other's spirits with humor and teasing, especially when the other was disheartened. For the last ten years it had just been the two of them. They'd lost their mother when Bridget was five and their da when she'd turned thirteen. Neighbors had been there to help out with their small farm, but Dermot and his best friend Sean had done the brunt of the heavy work, leaving the gardening, feeding, and milking to Bridget.

"You must understand, Dermot, Sean's like a brother to me."

"And me as well." Her brother's sigh was heavy. "He'd treat you well, Bridget."

"Aye, but he doesn't love me," she whispered.

"And how would you be knowing that?" Dermot demanded.

She shrugged. How could she put into words what she'd sensed and felt, so that her brother would understand? He was too tied to their family farm to even see that Megan would marry him in a heartbeat if he'd but ask.

"I just know."

Dermot's eyebrows raised up, and he waited for her to explain how she knew. When she remained silent, he turned and started to walk away. "I've work."

"As always," she whispered, wishing her hard-headed brother would look beyond the nose on his face and see the possibilities waiting for him before they disappeared like the image in the lake and rainbow above it.

As her brother's hand was lifting the latch, she called out to him. He stopped and waited, but didn't turn around, when she said, "I heard Thomas Skinner was over at the flower shop yesterday."

Her brother's entire body went taut, and still he didn't turn around. "And?" his voice was deceptively soft.

"I hear he plans on wooing Megan with promises of taking her across the Atlantic."

Her brother seemed to crumple in on himself. "What could I possibly offer Megan then?" he whispered, opening the door.

"Your foolish heart and your hard head," she called out, but her brother didn't stop. He kept on walking, head down and shoulders slumped.

Following behind her brother and Sweeney's lorry, Bridget walked to Dr. Murphy's clinic. When she opened the door, she knew Duncan had come around; his curses were loud enough to be heard back at the pub.

"Well then," she said smiling at Dr. Murphy's eldest daughter, and assistant, Nuala. "The patient must be feeling better."

Nuala's eyes danced with humor. "Da has a special way with patients."

Bridget nodded and wondered why she'd come. Duncan wouldn't have wanted her to, would he? She hugged her arms tightly about herself and walked over to the window. The street was deserted; as well it should be this time of day. Most of the residents of their village were hard at work, looking forward to a bracing cup of tea in another hour or so.

By then, more residents would wander on down to the pub, being Friday evening and the end of the work week for some. For others, those with farms and the like, there was always work on any day of the week.

"Are you here about the Yank?" Nuala asked, after a brief spate of typing on her computer keyboard.

Bridget shrugged.

"Well, the only other patient is Old Mr. Reilly, and I can't imagine that his wife'd be pleased to have you asking after himself. Mrs. Reilly being a mite jealous of her man, even after fifty-five years wed."

Bridget turned from the window and smiled. "She does worry overmuch, doesn't she?"

The two shared a few moments of local gossip until the door to the examining room opened swiftly and then closed. Michael and Patrick were trying to slip out of the doctor's office without being questioned by Bridget. That was their first mistake.

Thinking they'd made it to the outside door without incident was their second.

"What did you give Duncan for his aching head?" Bridget demanded of the older Sweeney brother.

Michael shrugged and looked at Patrick. When neither one answered, Bridget felt her temper begin to boil. "I don't think Dermot or Sean hit him all that hard," she began, only to be interrupted by Michael.

"Your brother has a mean streak in him, make no mistake," Michael said. "But Sean, well, he's just plain crazy."

Patrick nodded vigorously, looking from his brother to Bridget and back.

She knew it was true and didn't argue because she wanted to ask him about the pills he'd given Duncan.

Michael walked over to where she stood halfway between the window and the front door and took her hands in his. "My cousin is a stubborn man. You should know that from the start."

"Aye," Bridget said, then waited, sensing there was more Michael had to say.

"He's been hurt, recently."

"Anyone with eyes can see the bruises."

"For the love of God, woman," Michael exclaimed. "Let me finish."

She clamped her jaw shut and kept a tight hold on her temper.

"He won't thank me for telling you." Michael looked over at Patrick. The other man nodded and Michael turned back to Bridget.

Her eyes narrowed on the man in front of her, not daring to say another word, worried that Michael would simply leave without telling her the whole of it. Her patience was well rewarded.

"He was injured on the job…badly."

"What does he do when not stocking your pub?" she asked.

"He was a policeman…a detective in Boston."

"Was?"

"Aye." Michael's entire demeanor changed. "After he was shot—"

"Shot?" Bridget's stomach flipped and bile rose up her throat.

"Aye," Michael continued. "He'd just come home from the hospital…"

"And?" she prompted.

Michael looked over his shoulder at the closed door. "He was jilted. Three months ago, the woman he was to wed left the ring he'd put on her finger with a note on their kitchen table."

Bridget saw the compassion most people missed when first getting to know the elder Sweeney. She nodded, hoping to encourage more information from him.

"Duncan was devastated," he said simply. "He was just getting his strength back physically, and she pulled the rug out from under him, emotionally."

When Michael fell silent, Bridget thought he'd finished. He wasn't. "She was the love of his life."

"Not bloody likely," Bridget mumbled just loud enough for Nuala to hear. The other woman's eyes widened, but she didn't utter a sound.

"What was that?" Michael asked.

She shook her head at him. "Nothing."

"I've known you half your life, Bridget," he said. "It was definitely not nothing."

When she thought he'd prod her further, he surprised her by grabbing her by the upper arms and bringing her close. He kissed her forehead and hugged her tight. "Please don't tell him I told you."

Surprised by Michael's show of emotion, she blurted, "Why did you?"

"Duncan needs someone to love him, for who he is, not who he could be, or was."

"But I—"

Michael motioned to Patrick, "We've a pub to run." He doffed his cap to the ladies and pushed Patrick out the door.

Bridget couldn't help but wonder if Duncan would ever willingly speak to her again.

Chapter 6

Duncan ground his teeth in an effort to keep the room from spinning. The doctor had just finished his examination and was shaking his head.

"You need rest, preferably bed-rest."

"My cousin needs me over at the pub." Duncan began rising up off the examination table and stumbled.

"And a lot of good you'll do Michael or Patrick when they find you beneath a keg in the back room or basement," the doctor admonished, using a steadying hand to keep Duncan from cracking his skull.

"But I'm needed," Duncan started to say. One look at the doctor, and he clamped his mouth shut.

"That's better," Doc Murphy said with a nod. "Now, I'll be telling you what you need to do, lad."

Duncan hunched his shoulders. Truth be told, he was tired. His jaw ached, his eye hurt, and his knuckles, well, best not to look at them again for another day or so, until the swelling and bruising went down. But unlike his cousins, he didn't have a sweetheart waiting down the lane to soothe his aches and pains and offer kisses along with a stiff shot of whiskey.

"I understand there's someone outside to see you," the doctor said.

Duncan's head snapped up, and he immediately regretted the action. "Who?"

"Why don't I just send her in, and you can see if you won't change your mind about resting after all." Doc Murphy handed him a written prescription and told him to have it filled if the pain became too intense, but warned it would make Duncan sluggish.

"Any more than whatever Michael gave me?"

The doctor grinned. "Not overmuch."

Duncan shook his head. "No thanks. I prefer knowing what's going on around me and will settle for aspirin with a whiskey chaser."

"Come and see me if your vision starts to blur, or the headache doesn't go away."

"Thanks, Doc." Duncan had seen the old physician during an earlier trip to Ireland and had liked him then. It wasn't the doctor or his orders that irritated the heck out of him; it was the source of his injuries. He'd spent too long recuperating from that last one.

"Come right on in," Duncan heard Doc saying to someone, as he struggled to button his shirt with his mangled hands.

His heart stuttered to attention the moment Bridget O'Halloran slipped into the examining room.

"What do you want?" He didn't know what prompted him to ask her again, since she hadn't answered him before.

He sounded rude and knew she'd thought so too, by the dark expression clouding her pretty face. But he didn't have time for women, not after— *No*, he thought. Don't go there right now. He hadn't thought of Melanie in three days, or was it four?

Now that he had, he could see her face clearly as she yanked the diamond from her hand and slammed it onto the table alongside the note she'd left for him. *No,* he shook his head, that wasn't right. His brain was still just a bit foggy from the painkiller Michael had slipped him. *Wasn't he the fool thinking his cousin had given him aspirin?*

He hadn't been there to witness the returning of the ring or the writing of the scant few words she'd written. "*I'm leaving. Melanie.*"

"I thought you might need a lift back to the Sweeney's, since your cousins left you here."

Her offer seemed sincere.

"Where are Dermot and his knuckle-dragging buddy?" Duncan demanded, looking behind Bridget as if expecting to see them.

"Not here," she whispered, taking a step closer. "I'm so sorry, Duncan, I never meant for them to—"

Seeing the anguish in her whiskey-colored eyes, he raised his hand. "Just let it go. It's done."

Her eyes glistened with tears threatening to spill over. "But they hurt you."

Duncan called himself a fool and worse, but in the end, couldn't help himself. He reached out and caught the first tear that fell, then brushed it away with the tip of his finger. "I've had worse injuries playing soccer."

"Soccer?"

"You know the game with eleven players and the round black and white ball they try to kick into the goal?"

He was teasing her, and she must have sensed it. She looked up at him, hope shining in her tear-bright eyes. He was definitely going to regret this. It would be his last thought as insanity gripped him by the shoulders and shook every last lucid thought from his aching head while his heart drifted toward the lovely Irish lass.

"You mean football?" she asked.

He grinned. "Is that what you Irish call it?"

Her smile was brief, fleeting. "Are you sure I cannot give you a lift?"

Duncan groaned, knowing he was going to give in. "Where did you park your car?"

"Car?"

"Isn't that how you were going to give me a lift?" he wondered how else she could accomplish it, unless she had a magic broom stashed behind the bushes out front.

"Oh!" her hands flew to her cheeks. They flushed in embarrassment as she realized she'd walked, leaving her car at the pub. "I'll be right back," she told Duncan. Turning toward Nuala, she instructed, "Don't let him leave until I get back with the car."

Nuala just smiled, nodded, and kept typing.

Duncan sat on the nearest chair and prepared to wait, expecting dark-eyed Nuala to continue to work while he did.

The woman surprised him by stopping to smile at him. "How would you like to help me snag the man of my dreams?"

Duncan's groan echoed her lilt of laughter. "Why me?"

"You're perfect," she told him.

"What's so perfect about me?" he demanded, edgy with pain and aggravated by the events of the day.

"Now that you're here and Bridget is convinced you're the man she's supposed to marry…"

"Now hold on," he said. "I didn't agree to marry anyone."

"Umm, hmm," she nodded. "All right, then, but at least Sean will see that Bridget is really serious and has been all this time."

"Sean?" Duncan closed his eyes and slumped against the back of the chair. "Dermot's friend?"

"One and the same."

He couldn't believe the petite chestnut-haired beauty could be interested in the behemoth Mulcahy. "What do you see in him?"

"He's so gentle, and he has this little dimple when he smiles."

Duncan's head reeled. Way too much information. "But that doesn't explain—" he began.

"I love him," she interrupted.

"You love him?" he repeated, hoping he'd heard wrong.

"With all my heart."

He stared long and hard at the woman, and still the expression on her face didn't change. She meant what she said. She loved the guy. "Why should I help you?" he finally asked.

"That way, you can have Bridget all to yourself, while I soothe Sean's bruised ego and convince him that I've loved him for years."

"And have you?" Duncan demanded, remembering the faithless

Melanie who hadn't stuck around long enough to see if he'd lose his leg or keep it.

Her eyes misted, and he was afraid she'd cry. "Don't start," he said, rising unsteadily to his feet.

She jumped to her feet and was at his side before his head cleared. "Easy now, you shouldn't try to move so quickly until the painkillers wear off a bit."

"Get yer hands off Nuala!"

The now-familiar roar bounced off the waiting room walls. *Twice in one day?* The odds were pretty much in Mulcahy's favor that he would either maim Duncan for life or end it with a few well-placed punches.

"And why would you care?" Nuala demanded, holding Duncan closer to her, shifting so her bounteous bosom pressed against him and nearly had his eyes crossing.

The sharp report of skin meeting skin echoed in the room. Sean's head snapped back and his eyes narrowed. "Why in heaven's name did ye do that, Nuala?"

"Because, you big baboon, I didn't want you to hit poor Duncan again. You've already addled his brains enough for one day, and another blow to the head just might kill him."

To Duncan's shock, Sean's face lost every ounce of color. One minute Duncan was being held against Nuala, and the next was shoved into a chair while she supported Sean, leading him over to the two-seater sofa on the opposite wall.

"What about—" Duncan began, only to stop when he saw that Mulcahy looked as if he'd run face first into a wall. Stunned would be the best description.

"Sean?" Nuala murmured, stroking his face and combing her fingers through his wavy red hair. "Are you all right?" she asked. "You aren't going to be sick are you?"

Mulcahy shook his head, but still looked a little green to Duncan. Even if he wanted to tell them what he thought, neither one of them were paying him any attention. Sean's eyes were glued to Nuala's, and hers were glued to Sean's. He wondered now if what had happened had been planned or simply fate intervening before he had a chance to agree to help the woman.

Nuala pressed her lips to the big man's cheek and looked over her shoulder at Duncan. When she winked at him, he knew it had all been part of the woman's plan. Interesting, the man claimed to love Bridget, yet Bridget told Mulcahy, in front of her brother no less, that he didn't love Bridget, he just thought he did.

But if he could lay odds, he'd guess that Nuala really loved the big guy. Sean seemed willing to consider all of the attention and sweet-looking kisses Nuala showered all over his face and neck as his due. *Lucky guy.*

"Nuala, I wouldn't ever mean to hurt anyone," Mulcahy rasped.

"And don't I know it for a fact then, Sean," she soothed.

Mulcahy groaned before yanking Nuala close.

"Er, I'll just wait outside," Duncan said, although no one seemed to be listening.

When he stepped outside, his head felt just a bit clearer for being out in the fresh air. He leaned against the brick front of the office and crossed his legs at the ankles, waiting for his ride.

Bridget drove up a few minutes later, flushed and obviously distraught that he hadn't waited for her inside.

"Nuala and Sean needed some privacy," he said, nodding toward the window.

Bridget looked in the partially opened window and gasped. "Nuala?" Her friend jolted and dragged her lips from Mulcahy's long enough to smile at Bridget and wave at Duncan. Then she placed her hands on either side of the big man's face and kissed him for all she was worth.

"Well, then," Bridget said, her face turning a delightful shade of pink. "We'd best get goin'."

Duncan studied the way she held herself just far enough away from him so that their bodies didn't touch and wondered what had caused her change of heart. Earlier, she'd all but thrown herself at him. *Had she changed her mind?*

He couldn't say why it bothered him, but his gut told him he'd better figure out what was going on inside Bridget's head. "We don't have to go straight back to the pub, do we?"

Chapter 7

Bridget wasn't sure just what had happened in the doctor's office after she'd left to get the car, but something momentous had occurred. Nuala and Sean were wrapped around each other like a vine, and wasn't that a grand thing?

She'd known of Nuala's feelings for Sean for years. Maybe now, Sean would look beyond the end of his nose and see what could be, instead of what he thought he wanted. He was a good man, and a good friend, but she didn't love him like she loved Duncan.

Lord, and how was that possible? They'd just met—albeit under extraordinary circumstances. Could love happen in a heartbeat?

"Where would you like me to drive you, then?" she asked, hoping he wouldn't want to go too far. With his injuries, she didn't want to be too far from Doc Murphy.

Duncan looked at her and tilted his head to one side. "Do I make you nervous?"

If only you knew, she thought.

He grinned at her, and something deep inside clicked open. Feelings kept under lock and key, since first her mother, and then her father died, swept through her. She didn't know whether to laugh or cry, as conflicting emotions rioted through her, making her head hurt and her heart reel.

She closed her eyes so he wouldn't see that tears were just a moment away. She'd already cried in front of him, hadn't she? Lord, she couldn't think, but she could feel.

Why him? she wondered, opening her eyes. *Why now?*

Lord above, why hadn't he left her to drown?

"Bridget," he rasped, wrapping his arm about her, leading her over to the car. "I'm supposed to be resting," he said. "Any ideas of how to accomplish that?"

She couldn't hold back the laugh that escaped. "Dozens," she said, "but none that would be appropriate, given the fact that you aren't interested in marrying me, and I'm saving myself for the man I'm to wed."

That shut him up while he held her door open and then got in the passenger side of the car. She turned the key in the ignition and slowly pressed on the accelerator.

While they talked about Nuala and Sean and his Sweeney cousins, her mind wandered. Where could they go to guarantee that he'd rest? A few minutes outside of the village and she knew.

The ring of stones up in the distance called to her. Bridget drove toward them until they ran out of road. "Come on," she urged, getting out of the car. She'd been drawn to the ancient place, strengthened by the vibrations humming in the air around the half circle of standing stones.

Duncan caught up to her in a few strides. "Where are we?"

" 'Tis old enough not to have a name."

"What does everyone around here call it?" His interest was a balm to her uneasiness. Did he feel the power, too?

"Padraig's Ring."

"And?" he prompted, offering his hand as they drew closer to the ring.

The stones rose before them and she breathed deeply. "Do you feel it?" Tingles skimmed along her arms, and a feather-like caress touched her cheek. The ancients were giving their blessing. She smiled at him.

Lightning flashed, thunder boomed, and the air crackled around them. Duncan shoved Bridget to the ground and covered her body with his, protecting her.

"Don't move! I've felt this sort of electrical charge before," Duncan warned. "I lost three friends on a soccer field ten years ago when lightning struck from an innocent looking sky just like this one."

The vibrations humming in the air were now at her back. When Duncan pushed up to check the sky, she rolled over so they were face to face.

Fate. Destiny. There were Druid priestesses in her bloodline, and she knew from the depths of her being that here and now was where she was supposed to be. Duncan was fated to be her mate. She wrapped her arms around him and urged him closer so she could hear the steady beat of his heart.

***

Duncan's head spun and his heart hammered against his ribs. Fear for their safety was clouded by the scent and feel of the woman in his arms.

He tried to move away from her, but the ground started vibrating. The need to protect her had him tightening his hold and shifting so his back was on the ground. He looked up, but the clouds that had been gathering and disbursing electrical charges into the air around them had dissipated.

Confusion reigned. "Where are the clouds?"

Bridget's gaze locked with his. "They've gone. What you're feeling is the power of Padraig's Ring."

Duncan's time on the force had taught him that some cases were solved with more than logic, facts, and reason. Relying on his gut instincts and a healthy dose of luck helped balance out logic, fact and reason.

Right now his gut told him to trust Bridget and the ancient magic sizzling in the air inside the stones. A smart man knew when to stand and fight and when to give in.

His gaze focused on the shape of her mouth, remembering the softness of her lips. He didn't fight the urge; he gave in to the temptation and kissed her. Gently. Tentatively.

When she kissed him back, his heart yearned for more than it had ever had before. She drew something out of him he hadn't known still existed. He wanted—no—needed Bridget in his life.

"Bridget," he rasped, pulling her close and breathing deeply. Contentment filled him as her head rested against the hollow of his shoulder and he drifted off to sleep.

The air warmed around them as they lay on the soft moss in the center of the half-ring of ancient stones. Bridget sighed knowing that only those fated, destined to be together, were accepted in Padrig's Ring.

She fell asleep with a prayer of thanks on her lips.

Chapter 8

Duncan woke with a jolt, and for a heartbeat couldn't remember where he was or why he had been sleeping within a half-ring of stones.

The woman in his arms woke slowly and smiled. "We've been blessed," she whispered.

He wasn't sure if she referred to the fact that lightning hadn't struck them while they slept, or if she meant that neither of them had drowned in the lake.

Before he could ask, she wrapped her arms around him and

buried her face against his chest and murmured something he couldn't quite hear.

"What?"

She stiffened in his arms and shook her head at him refusing to repeat herself.

The frustration and anger in her gaze caught him off guard. Experience had taught him that if he were about to be damned, he'd best know the reason why.

"I didn't hear what you said," he told her, "please tell me?"

She couldn't look him in the eye, but she managed to find her courage and said, "You didn't say you loved me."

Her words had his eyes closing as he pulled her back into his arms. Did he even know what love was? The same helpless feeling he'd experienced those first few days home from the hospital returned with a vengeance. "Love?" he murmured, remembering the stark black words Melanie had left behind with her engagement ring. "I'm not sure I'm ready to love someone else."

Duncan's honesty slashed through the feelings blossoming inside her and left her bleeding. " 'Tis a shame your heart's too puny to find any room in it for me."

She eased out of his embrace and walked toward her car. Without looking at the stones shimmering on either side of her, she called out, "If you want a ride, you'd best be coming along, then."

Duncan caught up with her as she was opening the car door. His hand closed over hers. She looked down at the size of it; though battered from defending himself, it was still a strong, well-shaped hand, twice the size of hers.

"If I could make myself," he rasped. "You'd be the one I'd love."

The laughter bubbling up inside of her was harsh and left a bitter taste in her mouth. "Sure, and that's a romantic thing every woman wants to hear from the man she loves."

His eyes narrowed as he stared down at her. "If you can't accept me for who I am, then there's no point in even having this conversation."

"Well, now," she whispered. "His first truth of the day."

With that, she tugged her hand free, opened the door the rest of the way, and slid onto the seat. Not even looking to see if his hand was free of the doorframe, or still gripping it, she slammed it shut.

She put the car into reverse and gunned the engine as Duncan slid onto seat beside her. "You could have broken my hand."

Her eyes met his, and for a moment, she let everything she felt for him flow through her. From the combination of confusion and heat in his gaze, she knew he understood but couldn't accept what she hadn't been able to put into words.

With the toss of her head, she shoved the bubbling emotions back into the tidy box in the back corner of her heart and closed the lid. "I've finished waiting, boy-o."

The ride back to the village was silent, and it pleased Bridget to know that the man beside her was as irritated as she. *Good*. 'Twas about time someone besides herself was unhappy with the choices life had tossed in their path.

"I'll just drop you by Sweeney's Pub, then. Shall I?"

Without waiting for his agreement, she skidded to a stop outside the front of the pub and waited until she heard the door open and close. Not looking to see if his big feet were in the way of her back tires, she gunned the motor again and put the car in drive.

***

"Well, then, Patrick," Michael said from just inside the pub's open door. "Himself's back and in a temper."

Duncan ignored them, pushing his way into the pub and headed toward the back where the delivery would be waiting for him to unload it.

"Should we tell him not to overdo it?" Patrick asked.

Michael shook his head. "I'm thinkin' he needs to lose himself in physical labor, either that or a good clean fistfight."

Patrick nodded and walked back over to the bar where a few patrons had gathered for their first pint of the day.

He added the last bit of Guinness to the three pint glasses he'd been building, and with a flourish and twist of his wrist, wrote the letter 'S' on each one in the creamy foam.

"Does anyone here fancy a go at our American cousin?"

The loud laughter filled Patrick's heart and hopefully eased some of the tension in his cousin's shoulders. Judging from the set of them as Duncan had made his way into the back, his cousin wouldn't be coming out for a couple of hours.

"Michael?"

His brother paused in his conversation on the other side of the pub. "Aye?"

"Maybe we should see if Megan's got a few moments now that the flower shop's closed for the day."

Michael nodded. "Bridget'll need a friend to talk to."

Conversation lagged and he knew most, if not all, of the patrons heard. In a village the size of theirs, good news—or bad—traveled fast.

Chapter 9

Duncan hammered his hand against the side of the crate he'd emptied, breaking the slats. "Love," he ground out. "What the heck does she know about love?"

"More than ye know, lad," a deep voice rasped from behind him.

Duncan spun about, fists raised, but no one was there.

"Great, now I'm hearing voices," he mumbled. "Michael's gonna regret giving me those painkillers."

" 'Tisn't yer cousin's fault that ye've a head of granite and a heart to match."

He spun around for the second time, and saw the air shimmer and take form in the far corner of the cellar. He blinked, but the image of a transparent man remained floating just a foot above the packed dirt floor.

"Ye aren't seeing things, lad," the man cackled. "I'm real enough."

"Jesus, Mary, and Joseph!" Duncan made the sign of the cross. "You're not real."

"I was once."

"There's no such thing as ghosts." Duncan flexed his hands,

reached for a bit of the broken box, and walked slowly toward the corner.

"Then ye won't be needin' that bit of wood to swipe at me with."

The ghost had the grit to grin at him. Duncan stopped in his tracks and closed his eyes. "I'm imagining this. It's the combination of Dermot's right cross and Michael's painkillers."

"Believe whatever makes ye feel better, lad," the ghost said. "But ye'd best believe that I'm standin' here right in front of ye."

Duncan opened his eyes. The ghostly figure was still there. Digging deep for his floundering courage, he said, "Okay, if you really are here, there must be a good reason. I've been in the cellar dozens of times, and I've never seen you before."

The ghost nodded and smiled at him. "Well now, aren't ye the clever lad."

"I'd like to think so."

"If ye must know why I'm here—"

Duncan took a step back and folded his arms across his chest. waiting.

" 'Tis what happened today in the Ring of Padraig."

Shock held him in rooted to the dirt floor. How did the ghost know he'd been there?

"How do you know—" he began, only to be interrupted by the ghost.

"I'm not chained to one place, ye know."

Duncan frowned, "How would I? You're the first ghost I've ever seen, let alone talked to."

"Well then, shall we raise a glass of the Irish together?"

Duncan scrubbed his hands over face and winced in pain. "Sure." He really needed a drink.

Walking over to the shelf beneath the staircase, he reached up and pulled down a bottle from his cousin's personal stash—twenty-five year old Irish Whiskey. "This ought to do it."

When he turned around, the ghost was floating right in front of him. "No need to use a glass, lad. Just give it here."

Although Duncan thought it would be a waste of first class whiskey if the bottle slipped through the ghostly fingers reaching for it, he held it out.

But the bottle didn't pass right through the ghost's hands. With each pounding beat of Duncan's heart, the ghost grew less transparent. The bottle rested against lips that looked as real as his own.

When the ghost had swallowed enough to satisfy himself, he swiped his sleeve against his mouth and handed the bottle back to Duncan. His hands weren't quite steady as he accepted it.

"Ahh, 'tis me comin' and goin' out of focus that has yer back up, then?"

Duncan could only nod. This day had been filled with highs and lows. The high point being…

"About Bridget—" the ghost began, and Duncan nearly dropped the bottle he held to his lips. *Could the spirit read his thoughts?*

"She's me great-granddaughter and close to me heart."

Perfect, the ghost knew they'd been to Padraig's Ring, but why that should bother the spirit, he had no idea. It wasn't as if he'd seduced Bridget and had his way with her. From the moment they'd stepped inside the ring, he'd felt the magical currents zinging around them, as if they were bouncing off the stones.

When they'd fallen on the soft bed of moss, he'd pulled her close and felt an utter sense of peace surrounding him. Lulling him to sleep. The next thing he remembered was jolting awake with Bridget still wrapped in his arms.

He set the bottle down, out of harm's way, and waited to hear what the ghost would say next.

"If the Ring accepted ye, allowing ye inside it unharmed, then ye've not a thing to worry over, lad. She's fated to ye. As long as ye marry her, naught that's bad will happen to ye."

Duncan's head snapped up, and he bit out, "I'm not marrying anyone."

The ghost held out his hand for the bottle. Duncan picked it up and gave it back to him. Once again, the ghost's form became more solid as the bottle touched his mouth. After a long swallow, the ghost sighed deeply and nodded. "That would be a pity, lad, because she's a treasure to be sure."

Duncan's head began to spin. When he'd pulled her from the lake, he'd thought—

"Ahh," the ghost interrupted Duncan's thoughts. "So ye have feelin's for the lass."

Duncan tried to sort through the morass of feelings swirling around inside him, finally admitting, "Yeah. I guess I do."

"Well then," the ghost said, clapping a hand to Duncan's shoulder. "Then it's pleased I am to meet ye." He held out an opaque hand.

Duncan couldn't say just why he reached for it to clasp in his own, must have been what was left of the painkillers in his system. But what shocked him to the bone was the solid grip the ghost had.

"Name's Dermot O'Halloran."

"Dermot?"

"Aye. Her brother's named for meself." The ghost grinned again. "Fine strappin' lad, isn't he?"

Duncan had to agree. The man had a right cross that had knocked him off his feet, and his friend Sean—

"That would be Mulcahy," Dermot cackled. "Those two have been trouble since me grandson died and left them to fend for themselves."

A bit more about the O'Hallorans began to make sense. "Then Mulcahy would be?"

"Best friend and surrogate brother to Bridget. 'Tis why she cannot consider Sean as a husband." The ghost tapped his forefinger to his chin. "It would have been a perfect match, but not in her mind, ye see?"

"I think I do." Duncan finally managed to get the bottle back and took a swig. It burned pleasantly all the way to his empty gut.

"I think ye need a wee bit more."

Duncan nodded and took another swallow. "You can't get whiskey this smooth back home."

"And why would we be exportin' the best of what we brew?"

Laughter bubbled up, surprising him. He hadn't laughed since…

"Melanie," the ghostly Dermot finished Duncan's thought for him.

"How did you know?"

"Ah, I've been around and visitin' our kin on the other side of the Atlantic a time or two."

Duncan's thoughts drifted to Melanie and the ghost added, "She wasn't the one for you. Bridget is."

"But I'm not kin, so how do you know about me or Melanie?" he demanded.

"Och, to be sure, I knew ye'd be makin' yer way over to Sweeney's and wanted to make certain sure that ye were deservin' of me Bridget."

Duncan's eyes grew wide with wonder. Had a keg rolled over on top of him and knocked him out cold? Was he dreaming or having an out of body experience?

"No. No and no," the ghost said. "If ye followed the fey out to the lake in time to rescue me great-granddaughter, then—"

"I didn't follow anyone," he began, then stopped short. But he had. Hadn't he?

"Ye had a feelin' in yer gut, lad that led you to Killarney Lake."

Duncan raked a hand through his hair. "I guess I did."

"Well, then. Now that that's settled, what else troubles ye and keeps ye from declarin' yer love for me lass."

"I can't marry anyone."

The ghost hovered closer, "And so ye've said, but ye know in yer heart that she's the one, don't ye?"

"I don't know." Duncan sat down on the stool by the back wall. "My brain hurts."

"Sure, and it's himself's right cross behind the pain, lad."

"I'm going crazy," Duncan said, dropping his head into his hands.

"Yer sane enough," the ghost said as he drifted back to the corner. "A bit on the slow side though."

"Wait!" Duncan called out when he noticed the figure fading into the wall. "What am I supposed to do now?"

"Tell her ye love her, lad," the ghost advised. "Marry her."

Duncan blinked and the ghost was gone. He walked slowly over to the corner, touched the damp stone wall, and shuddered. "I'm losing my mind."

He shook his head, turned on his heel, and walked back over to where he'd left the broken crate, but it was in one piece. Not broken.

"I couldn't let Sweeney think less of ye for breakin' his blasted crate, now could I, lad?"

Though there was no body to go with the voice, Duncan knew it was old Dermot O'Halloran. "Umm, thanks."

"Go to her, lad," the raspy voice urged. "Don't let her doubt yer feelin's."

***

Bridget opened the door and frowned at the woman standing on her doorstep. "Dermot's not here."

Megan looked at her and shook her head, "I know. I'm not looking for your thick-headed brother."

"Oh," was all she managed to reply before Megan pushed past her into the cottage. "I've come to talk to you about Duncan."

"There's nothing to talk about."

Megan walked through to the kitchen and made herself at home, lighting the burner under the teapot.

"I'm thinking there might be, if you're feeling as put out as he is."

"How would you know?"

"Michael called a little while ago," Megan explained. "You don't have to tell me anything you don't want to, but I'm here to listen in case you do."

Bridget wondered if it would help as she walked over to the cupboard where she kept the good teacups. Opening the door and reaching for them, she said, "There's a bit of soda bread and a few currant scones left from breakfast."

"Either'd be grand."

While Bridget set out their small snack, Megan told her, "I'm not sweet on Tom Skinner, you know."

Bridget was surprised Megan was even talking about the man who was trying to woo Megan away from Dermot.

"Sure and he's sweet on you, Meg." The whole village knew how Tom felt about the woman, and for that matter, how Dermot felt about Megan.

Megan smiled. "Well, that'd be too bad for him, as it's your hard-headed brother I love."

As soon as the words were out of her friend's mouth, Bridget felt relief wash over her. She'd sensed it, but was glad to have Megan confirm what

Bridget had felt. "He's afraid that Tom will whisk you across the Atlantic."

Megan tilted her head to one side. "Tom's hinted that he wants to."

"But?" Bridget prompted, hoping Megan wouldn't break her brother's heart and follow the elusive dreams so many had tried to find across the ocean and far from their homes.

"I don't love Tom," Megan said. "Why would I go?"

"Dermot thinks he isn't good enough for you," Bridget said in a low voice, getting up to flick off the burner and pour hot water into the waiting pot. "So why would you stay?"

"I can't help loving your brother, Bridget," Megan said, accepting the cup of tea Bridget placed in front of her.

"Why don't you tell him?"

"I have."

"Oh…then why—"

"Probably for the same reason Duncan Garvey hasn't realized that you and he are perfect for one another and meant to be together."

Bridget stared down at her cup. "He doesn't love me."

"Is that what he said?"

She almost answered that it was, but then she realized that he hadn't quite said that. "Actually, he said he wasn't ready to love someone else."

"Ah." Megan smiled at her. "Well then," she said, reaching for a scone and pausing before taking a bite. "It's a short trip from not ready to ready."

"But what about Dermot?"

The other woman finished chewing, picked up her cup, and sipped from it before answering. "I'm thinking I'll let him stew over Tom Skinner just a bit more before I put my plan into action."

Intrigued, Bridget couldn't help but ask, "What plan?"

"Sabotage."

"I don't understand," Bridget said slowly. "He isn't interested in anyone else, so how could you sabotage anything?"

"It's himself he's fighting and his own feelings for me," Megan confided. "I'm just going to help him realize how much he cares and then dazzle him with passion."

Bridget laughed softly. "It wouldn't be my plan, but I'm thinkin' it'll work for the two of you."

"I hope he loves me as much as I love him," Meg whispered.

Bridget shook her head, and Megan's eyes filled with tears.

It was Bridget's turn to get up and hug her friend. "Don't cry, Meg," she urged. "I'm thinking he loves you more."

Chapter 10

"Are you finished yet?"

Duncan heard his cousin calling him, but couldn't quite wrap his head around what had happened here just moments before. *Had he imagined it? Should he tell anyone?*

No, he reasoned with himself. The ghost had urged him to believe it had happened. Hah! If he believed the ghost, he thought as he reached for the bottle of Irish whiskey, then he would be married before the month was out.

And would that be so bad? He asked himself.

Remembering the woman he'd thought was the love of his life, he shook his head. His thoughts fast-forwarded to Bridget. "Am I crazy?"

"Do you think he's slipped and fallen?" he heard Patrick ask from the landing above.

Wondering if he had lost his mind, he stared into the open bottle of whiskey.

"Duncan?" Michael called out again.

"He's fit as a fiddle," a deep voice called out from across the room.

"O'Halloran?" Duncan heard his cousin rumble a curse before asking, "Why can't he haunt someone else?"

Duncan chuckled. "Probably because he likes your whiskey better?"

Michael stomped his way down the steps with a flashlight in his hand. "Don't think I don't know where my best whiskey's gone, O'Halloran."

"Sure and it's a stingy man ye've become, lad," the ghost called out, though he still hadn't materialized.

Duncan wondered why he hadn't made an appearance yet.

Michael looked at Duncan and grabbed the bottle, though his eyes shifted over to the corner as he spoke. "Why can't you drink someone else's whiskey?"

"Because he'd miss out on the side benefit of keeping a watch over his kin," Duncan answered.

"Which kin?" Patrick demanded, coming to a halt beside his older brother.

"Bridget and Dermot," Duncan answered, watching the corner to see if the ghost would appear. After a few minutes more, he realized the ghost wasn't going to be making an appearance after all.

"Ah, so you've been up to Padraig's Ring, then?" Michael said slowly.

"What makes you think that?" Duncan asked.

Patrick chuckled. "You've a bit of moss and dirt stuck to your back which tells a tale all its own."

"You'd better stop there," Duncan warned his younger cousin.

"Fine then." Patrick held up his hands and backed away from Duncan. "Don't tell us about how sweet—"

Duncan's fist plowed into Patrick's jaw, and his cousin went down like a stone.

"Jesus," Michael swore, stepping in between Duncan and his brother. "He's just a kid, Duncan. Don't kill him because he's an *eedjit*."

Duncan swore and fisted his hands to keep from throttling Patrick.

"Nicely done, lad," the ghost materialized, floating just an inch above the dirt-packed floor. "Avenging the lass's honor."

"I wasn't—" Duncan began, only to be interrupted.

"Aye, ye were, and it gladdens me heart."

Michael took a full step backward. "O'Halloran!"

Patrick stirred slowly and sat up before struggling to his feet.

Duncan held the bottle of whiskey out to the ghost.

"Don't give him any!" Patrick warned, as the ghost reached out and once again his hand miraculously changed from transparent to solid.

"Ye've a good heart, Duncan," the ghost replied, tipping the bottle up and swallowing a mouthful.

"Ah." Swiping the back of his hand across his mouth, old Dermot smiled. " 'Tis time we spoke about the wedding, now that yer kin has arrived."

The other-worldly visitor's pronouncement threatened Duncan's sanity and shocked him enough to have him reeling a step back.

"Catch him before he keels over!" The ghost's gleeful tone snapped Duncan back to reality and the present.

"I'm seeing things," he said, turning to his cousins. "Aren't I?"

"If ye'd like to think so, I'll not tell ye different, lad," the old curmudgeon chuckled.

"I wish I could lie to you," Michael began.

"Please," Duncan ground out. "Feel free to lie to me. I'd rather not be seeing what I know can't be there or possibly exist."

"But lad—" the ghost began.

"I don't know how you know about where Bridget and I were earlier this afternoon," he said slowly, clenching his hands into fists. "But nothing happened, so I won't be bullied into marriage."

The ghost's face, mottled with rage just an inch in front of his own, had Duncan's breath whooshing out. "I—"

"Enough!" the ghost bellowed. Dust shook from the rafters and sifted down onto their heads.

"Ye've been to the sacred ring of stones with me darling great-granddaughter. The ancients have accepted ye. Yer fated and now ye'll hold up yer end of the bargain, me boy-o."

"I'm not—"

Before Duncan could protest a second time, the shelves on either side of them crashed to the floor. Whiskey and wine mingled in the dirt, forming fragrant glass-strewn puddles all around them.

"Shut your bloody mouth, Duncan!" Michael warned.

"But I—"

Two more liquor-laden shelves hit the dirt with a spectacular crash, and this time shards of glass flew toward him. Duncan raised his arms up, but not in time to prevent a trio of sharp-edged fragments from raking across his cheekbone.

Patrick shoved Duncan to the floor, and Michael straddled him in a stance worthy of a medieval warrior. "You're no longer welcome here, Dermot," Patrick shouted, standing back to back with his brother.

A cold wind swirled around them, but the Sweeneys stood their ground while mist formed in front of them.

"You'll not take out your anger on my cousin or any of our family," Patrick warned, his voice calm amidst the destruction surrounding them.

Duncan waited a few moments then started to push up off the floor, only to be shoved back down by Michael, who hissed a warning for him to be still.

"He'll not get away with ruining Bridget!" The ghost's voice rumbled from all four corners of the cellar.

"He didn't ruin her," Patrick said calmly as Michael motioned for Duncan to get up and stand behind him.

"Ye wee vermin!" Cold slapped against the trio as they stood with their backs together, fists raised to fight as they'd done a dozen years ago when the cousins had discovered Duncan being bullied out behind the pub one night.

As the floor beneath them began to rumble and bottles clinked together with the movement, Duncan called out, "I'll marry her!"

A hush settled over them, and for a heartbeat no one moved.

Duncan wasn't sure if the ghost had heard and fled, or if he was waiting for Duncan to say something else. Taking a chance, he stepped away from his cousins and held up his hand, motioning for them to stay where they were.

"Not that you care about anything but yourself, old man," Duncan said.

"Who said I didn't care?"

"If you cared about Bridget, you'd ask her how she feels about me." Duncan kept his voice deliberately even-toned. "Maybe she doesn't want to marry me."

The air around them dropped a few degrees before beginning to warm up.

"Ask her," Duncan suggested, brushing his hands on his pant legs. "If she'll have me, we'll be married by the week's end."

"But Duncan—" Patrick began.

"Hush, now," Michael warned.

"You're not such a bad lad," the ghost said, materializing one last time. With a wink and a tip of his tattered cap, he added, "For a Yank."

Warmth hit him in the face as the ghostly presence disappeared entirely. "Well," he said looking at his cousins. "And I thought trouble wouldn't be able to find me when I left Boston."

"You have no idea," Michael said, shaking his head.

"How are we going to re-stock and still pay for the shipment delivered earlier today?" Patrick looked around them at the damage.

"I'd be willing to bet O'Halloran would be amenable to re-stocking for us if I come through as promised and marry Bridget."

"As to that, Duncan," Michael began. "Neither Patrick or I would hold you to the promise you made to a ghost."

Duncan's stomach felt hollow. He really *had* talked to the long-dead spirit of someone who used to walk this earth. "I gave my word." And he'd keep it.

"But what about Bridget?" Patrick asked, as he started to sort through the piles of glass, wood, and rubble.

"I hope she's partial to whiskey cake and stout," Duncan grinned at his cousins. "I saw the cake in the freezer and know for a fact Guinness was delivered earlier today."

"That's not proper for a wedding." Michael shook his head.

"Ghosts making threats isn't my idea of a romantic beginning either," Duncan said, "but I'm willing to compromise."

Chapter 11

"Will I what?"

Bridget shook her head to clear it and stared at the dark-haired man standing before her. "I'm sorry, but could you repeat what you just said?"

Duncan's face looked as if it pained him. The bruises around his eye and along his jaw were dark purple.

Duncan's eyes narrowed. "Why, so you can go tell those blasted faeries that they were right?"

So she hadn't imagined it? He must have asked her, or else he wouldn't be so upset.

"I really wasn't listening, and please don't use that expression when speaking of the fey ones," she said, pausing to look over her shoulder. "They don't like it."

His expression changed, and the grin that lifted the corner of his beautifully sculpted lips tugged at her heart. Lord, he was handsome. Just like the image in the lake, well, except for the bruising and swelling.

His grin morphed into a smile that had him wincing. "Remind me not to smile until my face heals."

"Since it doesn't seem to be something you do on a regular basis," she snipped. "I don't think you'll need reminding."

He didn't answer her, but he did give her a stern look. As if that would deter her from speaking her mind. She'd told him plenty the day he dragged her out of the lake, he just hadn't believed half of what she'd said. If only she could get him to repeat his question.

Not knowing how else to get him to do so, since she'd asked nicely and he'd said rude things about the faeries, she simply crossed her arms in front of her and waited.

No man can hold out for long against the silent treatment.

"You're a stubborn woman, Bridget O'Halloran." Duncan started pacing in front of her, stirring up the dust she'd just swept off her front steps.

"Mind that you don't step on any of the gentry," she warned.

"The who?"

"Gentry," she said. "You know the little people." When he continued to stare at her, she racked her brain for a word that he'd associate with her meaning. "Leprechauns."

He stopped pacing and glared at her. "Great, just wonderful." He raised his eyes to the heavens. "I'm nearly killed by her brother and his knuckle-dragging friend, then a ghost tries to split my skull open with fifty bottles of whiskey and wine, and now that I'm asking—"

"Just what are you asking, Duncan Garvey?" Her patience was definitely gone. At his continued silence, she bit out, "And I'll remind you my brother and Sean didn't try to kill you, they were trying to protect my honor...and where did you see a ghost?"

He was back to staring at her again, in that extremely irritating way he had about him, like he was looking at a bug under a microscope.

"Sweeney's Pub."

She closed her eyes and swore.

His sharp crack of laughter surprised her. She opened one eye to see if he was still standing there, or if he'd walked away from her.

He stood a breath away from her. "I didn't think you'd know that particular expression."

She braced her hands against his chest and shoved.

Too bad he caught himself before his backside hit the ground. She fought against the urge to smile.

"Since you put it that way, I guess you really aren't trying to make me beg. Are you?"

She whirled around and slammed the door in his face.

"I'm thinkin' ye had yer chance, lad."

"Not now!"

Dermot's ghost began to materialize by the corner of the house where a morning glory vine clung tenaciously.

"What ails ye?"

"Nothing," Duncan bit out. "Not one blessed thing." He glared at the ghostly image. "At least not until I drove my cousin's car out to the lake and tried to do a good deed."

The ghost placed a hand to his chin and scratched it. " 'Tis the truth, you saved me Bridget's life."

"But that's not enough for you," Duncan snapped. "Is it?"

"There's no need for acting surly."

"Oh, but I think there is." He must have lost his mind. He was arguing with a ghost! Unable to let it go, Duncan spit out, "I asked your precious great-granddaughter to marry me, just like I said I would."

When the ghost floated without speaking, Duncan scrubbed his hands over his face and wished he hadn't.

"But she didn't answer ye."

"She sure as heck did," Duncan bit out. "She slammed the door in my face."

"That's not an answer," the ghost chuckled. "That's just temper talking."

Duncan shook his head. "Then I'm not listening." He started walking away.

"But what about Bridget?"

He stopped but didn't look over his shoulder. "I did what I said I'd do...I asked her."

"What about your promise to marry her?"

"He hasn't asked me yet!" Bridget yelled, leaning out the front window.

Duncan spun around and waited. "So you did hear me."

She shook her head, "Not really."

"What kind of an answer is not really?"

"The only one you'll get from me." Bridget slammed the window shut.

"You're not going about this properly," the ghost said, floating along beside Duncan as he stalked away from the thatched cottage with the pretty yellow door.

"Now there's news," he mumbled, kicking a stone with the toe of his boot.

"Ye've mortally wounded me!" a voice called out from a clump of violets at the side of the road.

"Well," the ghost snickered. "Now ye've done it."

The hair on the back of Duncan's neck stood on end. "Who said that?"

"The gentry me great-granddaughter warned ye to mind."

The ghost floated in a circle around him, until Duncan was dizzy and disoriented. Certain he was hearing things, his legs simply folded beneath him and he sat down—hard.

He dropped his head in his hands and tried to massage the ache away. It was no use. "Why did I have to come to Ireland?" he mumbled. "Why didn't I just stay in Boston and let Melanie cut out my heart with a spoon?"

"Even I know a spoon's not sharp enough." The odd little voice came from beneath his ear. He closed his eyes and vowed not to look.

"Ye'd best be taking a look at the lump ye've given poor Seamus," the ghost warned.

Duncan shook his head.

"Were ye tryin' to kill me entirely?" The voice sounded further away, closer to his knees now.

A hand slapping the back of his head had him opening his eyes wide. "What the heck?"

"Precisely where ye'll be headed, lad, if ye don't mind what yer kicking and where," O'Halloran's ghost warned.

"I really am dead," Duncan said with a sad shake of his head.

"Not from where I'm standin'," the ghost chuckled.

"So he's got the Irish in him, then," Seamus said, climbing up onto Duncan's knee.

"If I'm not dead, I've cracked my skull open and my brains have all fallen out." Duncan squinted at the little man perched on his jean-clad knee. "Because there is no way, I've got a…a…what are you, anyway?"

The little man drew in a breath and puffed out his chest with pride, "I'm a Leprechaun." Turning to his ghostly friend, he asked, "Jaisus, Dermot, doesn't the lad know anythin'?"

Duncan closed his eyes and counted to ten, but when he opened them, the ghost was hovering next to the tiny figure now standing on his knee. He didn't weigh much, but Duncan could feel the tiny heels of

Seamus's buckled shoes digging into his kneecap.

"The lad is having a hard time wrapping his addled wits about what I've said."

Seamus tilted his head to one side and nodded. "I can see that he is." He started walking up toward Duncan's pocket, and Duncan flinched.

The movement of his thigh muscle had the leprechaun diving for safety, clutching the wrinkle of jeans with both hands. "Lord, save us! Dermot," Seamus yelled. "Can ye not make the lad sit still until we've said our piece?"

"I'll try."

Duncan groaned. "No need. I'll sit still." He looked from the ghost to the little man dressed head to toe in shades of green and swore.

"I think he's finally understandin' the way of it, O'Halloran."

"Ye could be right," Dermot agreed.

"Well then, me name's Seamus O'Toole." The little man touched his fingertips to the brim of his hat. "I'd like to say I'm pleased to meet ye, but I'd be lyin' and would rather tell ye to watch yer step and mind where ye be kickin' stones."

Duncan rolled his eyes and fought the urge to sweep the irritating creature into the grass.

"I wouldn't if I were ye," the ghost warned.

Duncan shook his head. "I'll try to watch my step, Mr. O'Toole." And he would, good grief. He couldn't believe the stories his mother told him as a child were actually true!

"See that ye do, lad."

"Now, what about his problem?" the leprechaun asked O'Halloran.

"What problem?" Duncan demanded, tensing his body for a fight.

"Easy now," O'Halloran warned. "Sudden movement might just finish Seamus off entirely."

"Just spit it out, then." Duncan didn't have to dig deep for patience; his was gone.

"Ye gave yer word, boy-o," the ghost's voice was grave. "Yer not intendin' to go back on it now, are ye?"

Duncan shook his head. "I asked her once, I'm not asking again."

"But she didn't answer ye," the two other-worldly creatures said at the same time.

Duncan laughed. "She did."

"But I didn't hear—"

"She slammed the door in my face, and then slammed the damned window!"

"If she thinks about it long enough and hard enough," Duncan said slowly, "she'll realize that I've asked her to marry me and come looking for me."

The ghost looked at the leprechaun and then at Duncan. "Well then." He started floating away as the little man jumped off of Duncan's leg. "At least the lad has a plan."

"A poor one at that," Seamus grumbled."

"Bridget best be marryin' ye by the end of the week. Ye promised with yer kin as witnesses."

A cloud passed over the sun, and Duncan looked up at the sky. "Yeah well, we all know that…" the words dried up on his tongue. He was all alone, sitting by the side of the road, talking to himself.

"Damn."

"And mind what ye say in front of Bridget, lad," a distant voice called out in answer.

Chapter 12

"Then what happened?" Megan demanded.

"I slammed the window."

"Megan, darlin'," a deep voice echoed through the flower shop.

"Oh no." Megan's face flushed. "Don't move. Don't leave. Don't say a word!"

"But I—" Bridget fell silent at her friend's pointed look.

A tall man with wavy blond hair ducked his head and stepped into the back room. "How will your customers know where to find you," he asked, grinning down at Megan, "if you hide in the back room?"

"Uh…Tom," Megan rasped. "What a surprise."

"Is it now?" he tilted his head to one side, deepened his smile, and leaned down until his lips brushed the top of Meg's head. "And here I thought you knew I always keep my word."

Though Bridget didn't think it was possible, Meg's face turned a deeper shade of red. Meg's eyes beseeched Bridget to do something…anything. But she was at a loss for words, especially when Tom wrapped his arm around Meg's sturdy waist and pulled her into a passionate embrace.

"Meg," another voice called out from the front of the shop. "I've come to pick up the violets you've—"

Bridget's brother stepped into the back room, and his face lost all expression when he saw Megan McCourt plastered against the one man in town he hadn't beaten in a fistfight.

"Dermot," Bridget said loud enough to be heard three doors down. "Meg's just finishing up."

"I've eyes in my head, don't I?" Dermot ground out. "I can see she'll be far too busy for the likes of me."

Before Bridget could stop him, he spun on his heel and strode out of the shop.

"Did I ask you to kiss me?" Megan demanded, giving the big man a solid shove until he backed up a step.

"But I thought—"

Megan shook her head at him. "Not possible, when you haven't got a brain in your head!" She scooted around him and ran to the front of the shop.

The slamming of the front door had Tom shaking his head as if he'd been hit with something hard. "But I thought she'd—"

Sorry that the man had feelings for a woman who couldn't return them, Bridget patted his arm, then linked hers through his. "Have a walk with me then, Tom," she soothed. "And I'll tell you about the mischief my great-grandfather got himself into this morning."

Tom looked at her then. Deeply and for a moment, she wondered what Megan saw in Dermot when Tom Skinner was so obviously in love with Megan. "She doesn't love me," he rasped. "Does she?"

Bridget patted his arm and tugged him toward the front of the shop and out the door. "Let me tell you about the bottles of fine aged whiskey wasted."

"Bite your tongue!" Tom said, his eyes finally losing that sorrowful look in them. "No Irishman worth his salt would waste fine whiskey."

"Well now, I didn't say it was wasted entirely, did I?" she laughed, pulling Tom closer to her side. "Walk with me over to the pub, and I'll let Michael and Patrick tell their tale."

When a skeptical expression crossed his face, she laughed up at him. "Truly."

***

Duncan blinked then narrowed his eyes and swore. He rubbed his hand over his face and groaned. It would be awhile before the pain or bruising would go away.

But it would be longer still before his heart would recover from the sight of the fiery-haired woman with whiskey-colored eyes snuggling up to the blond-haired giant of a man as if she hadn't a care in the world, or had professed that she'd marry Duncan and no other just two days before.

"First Melanie, and now Bridget.

"I'm going home."

"Not unless ye want us to destroy that pub entirely." O'Halloran's ghost stood leaning against the corner of the flower shop, his tiny sidekick perched upon his shoulder.

"Not now," Duncan grumbled. "I've got enough problems."

"I take it ye've been back to the pub since we've seen ye last," O'Halloran said with a nod. "Have ye a plan to get rid of her then?"

Duncan didn't even try to figure out what the blasted ghost meant. "Her who?"

"The blonde beauty from across the foam," Seamus O'Toole answered with a sigh. "She'll steal yer breath, then break yer heart, that one."

Duncan knew then who had come to make his life a living hell all over again. "Melanie."

"Aye, that was the name yer cousin, Michael, called her by."

"Pretty enough," O'Halloran grumbled, "but doesn't hold a candle to my fiery-haired kin."

Duncan had no idea what he was going to do now.

In a flash, he remembered the way Bridget and the hulk of a man were walking arm and arm toward the pub. No way was he going to go to Sweeney's tonight. "Perfect...just perfect."

"Have ye a new plan, then?" the ghost asked.

"The old plan never would have worked," Seamus told him.

"Get lost; the two of you!"

"Well now," O'Halloran said, a smile forming on his ghostly lips as he watched Duncan striding toward the pub. "I'm thinkin' he's headed in the very direction he vowed not to go."

"Yer sharp as ever, Dermot," the leprechaun said with a grin. "Sharp as ever."

"Do ye think the lad will come out on top?"

"I've no doubt in me mind that he will," Dermot said with a grin. "But...it'll take some doing and some fancy-talkin' to convince both women he means what he says."

"I could use a spot of whiskey," Seamus said, using the ghost's arm as a slide and landing on his feet running. "I'll meet ye there."

The ghost nodded and vanished.

***

"And I'm sure he doesn't know that you're waiting to see him," Michael said, a frown creasing his brow. The woman standing in front of him was gorgeous. *Too gorgeous for the likes of him, or any other man she fancied for however long she planned to be faithful. And, according to what he'd heard from Duncan's mother, the blonde hadn't a faithful bone in her entire body.*

"Oh, but I'm sure Duncan—"

Bridget turned at the sound of his name. The breathy tone the bottle-blonde used made her skin crawl. "And how to do you know Duncan?"

The blonde narrowed her eyes for a moment then seemed to notice the big man standing beside Bridget, and the woman softened the frown into a beguiling smile.

Bridget didn't trust this one as far as she could throw her. Judging from the lack of meat on the woman's bony frame, Bridget figured she could toss the woman out the door and into the street and not even break a sweat. But maybe a few of the woman's spindly bones would break, Lord willing. She tried not to smile at the thought.

"Tom, why don't you go on back and ask Patrick about Dermot," Bridget urged. The last thing she needed was to worry about tripping over the man. But Tom wasn't moving. He was too busy staring at Melanie as if she were the creamy foam gracing the top of a freshly poured pint.

Tom started to say something, but the blonde smiled and said, "I'll be here for awhile, if you'd like to buy me a drink."

Perfect, Bridget thought. At least that would keep Tom away from Megan long enough to get her hardheaded brother back over to the pub.

Tom indicated that he would, just as the blonde gave him one of those irritating little waves with the tips of her fingers. *Did Yanks really do that sort of thing?* Bridget wondered. She'd thought it was just in the movies.

"Well now, honey," the blonde began, turning back to speak to Bridget.

"Seeing as how we've never met, you may call me Ms. O'Halloran," Bridget said with a decided edge in her voice. "And you are?"

"Duncan Garvey's fiancée. Melanie. Melanie Smith."

The bottom dropped out of Bridget's stomach and lay on the floor at her feet. The ache spearing through her middle had her squeezing her arms about herself.

"Here now, Bridget," Michael's voice sounded so far away. "Sit down now and put yer head between your knees." She could feel the pressure of his hand on the back of her head, forcing it down, a moment before her world went black.

"What happened?" Duncan demanded, walking into the pub and finding Bridget limp in his cousin's arms.

Michael nodded toward the end of the bar where a slender blonde sat sipping a Cosmo.

"Damn," Duncan growled.

"Don't swear when we've customers," Michael warned, pulling Bridget more securely in his arms. "I've got to get herself into the office; there's a couch there."

Duncan followed behind his cousin and damned himself every step of the way. He'd bungled this. Somehow he sensed it was his fault Bridget lay unconscious in Michael's arms. What had happened?

"When did Melanie get here?" he finally demanded as his cousin gently laid Bridget out on the sofa.

She was so pale he was afraid she'd fade into thin air, like her great-grandfather had more than once over the last day or so.

" 'Bout noon, I'm thinking," Michael answered. "Didn't you know she was coming?"

Duncan shook his head. "I haven't spoken to her since she broke it off," he said slowly. "I figured I'd never see her again."

"Apparently, your Melanie had a change of heart."

"Change in manicurists, change in hair stylists..." Duncan's voice trailed off as the woman on the couch stirred. He was at her side in a heartbeat. "Bridget." His voice wavered, and he knew then he'd been a fool to ignore the overwhelming feelings that had been building inside of him since the day he'd pulled her free from the depths of Lake Killarney.

"Mmmm..." she opened her eyes and then blinked. "Duncan," she said his name on a sigh. "What are you doing—" she stopped and closed her eyes. "What do you want?"

The change in her tone tipped him off to the fact that she'd remembered what had happened and who was downstairs sitting at the bar sipping a Cosmopolitan.

"Did you hit your head?" His worry increased when she didn't open her eyes and look at him.

She shook her head.

"Can you tell me what happened?" he urged, hoping she'd open her gorgeous eyes and look up at him. He reached for her hands, and he jolted as he gripped them. They felt like ice.

"You're sick." His statement was met with what sounded like a snort of disbelief.

"As if you'd be caring."

An invisible hand plowed into his gut at her words. But the pain was nothing compared to the sorrow in the depths of her eyes when she finally opened them and looked up at him. "Your Yank fiancée is waiting for you at the bar." She said each word as if it left a foul taste in her mouth.

It probably did, because hearing them left a noxious feeling in his aching stomach.

"Melanie and I are no longer engaged," he bit out. The words sounded like shots fired into an empty room, although their effect wasn't what he'd hoped. Bridget's eyes drifted closed again.

"Michael," she rasped, her voice sounding weaker than a moment before. "Can you please call Dermot and have him come get me."

His cousin's gaze met his, silently asking him what he was going to do about the woman lying listlessly between them. Duncan rubbed his eyes and struggled against the urge to smash his fists into something solid.

He mouthed the words, "I don't know."

"Duncan," a breathy voice called from just outside the door. "Are you in there?"

He swore and scrubbed his face with his hands, not caring that pain arrowed through his jaw. He welcomed it. Deserved it. "I'll be right back," he said, though neither Michael nor Bridget answered him.

Melanie walked toward him and wrapped herself around him. "I've missed you."

She tried to kiss Duncan, but he dodged her questing lips. "Why are you really here?" he demanded.

The blonde pouted, but he was immune to her little games. "And don't tell me you changed your mind, because that would be a load of crap, Mel."

Her blue eyes narrowed to angry slits of sapphire. "I hate when you call me that."

He grinned at her, "Yeah? Good, glad it still works."

"I thought you'd be happy to see me," she whined, swaying slightly.

Wonderful, she'd already had at least three cocktails if she wasn't quite steady on her feet. "Not in this lifetime, cupcake."

"Well aren't you just a pleasure—" she began, only to fall silent when he grabbed her by her arms and set her off to the side.

"If memory serves, you were the one who walked away from us, Mel," he said, continuing to use the nickname he liked and she hated. "You were generous enough to leave behind the ring you detested because it was too small and the key to our apartment. Which, by the way, you also told me was too small."

"But I've had time to think—"

"And so have I," Duncan interrupted. "You left me because you couldn't handle the thought of spending the rest of your life with a one-legged man."

He paused and drew in a deep breath. "That's when I realized that your leaving me was the best thing that could have happened to me."

"But, I—"

He ignored Melanie and kept talking, needing to get everything said. "Your leaving forced me to face what we'd both feared, that I'd lose my leg."

"But you didn't," Melanie said.

"By the grace of God, the skill of a gifted surgeon, and a hell of a lot of physical therapy."

What he'd realized during those pain-filled weeks returned full force. Though he said the words as gently as possible, he knew she wouldn't want to hear them, "I wasn't in love with you, Mel," he said softly, taking pity on her, knowing she'd probably never understand the reasons why he wouldn't be taking her back.

"I was in love with the image of you."

"Image?" she snipped. "What's wrong with that?" Her voice increased in volume as her temper got the better of her. "I've spent a lot of time and money to achieve this image."

Duncan smiled sadly, "And because you don't understand, it would never work."

"What—"

"Look, Mel. I never wanted you to lose so much weight that you'd endanger your health." When she huffed up, ready to speak, he continued. "And I sure as heck don't care if your hair is flawless blonde or a hundred different shades of brown and blonde mixed together."

Her eyes filled with tears as his words sank in. Finally.

"I prefer a woman who's comfortable in her own skin, not one trying to achieve her goal of the perfect image."

"But I'm not perfect," she started crying softly, her nose turning a bright red.

That sight made him smile. "It's okay not to be perfect, Mel."

"Then why can't you take me back?"

She really hadn't a clue. Probably never would.

"I'm sorry," he said at last. "But after you left, I realized one very important fact."

"What's that?" she asked sniffling.

He hated telling her, but knew he had to. "I was in love with the woman you were when I met you, not the new and improved version you kept trying to create."

"That's it, then?" she asked. "It's over?" she drew in a deep breath.

"Yeah," he said, looking over his shoulder to where his cousin and Bridget sat quietly talking. "That's it."

"Well," she said softly. "At least you were finally honest with me."

Her parting shot hit him right between the eyes. Hadn't he been honest with her from the start? Hadn't he told her he loved her generous curves, even though she dieted until she'd been hospitalized?

Hadn't he told her not to worry when she couldn't get the coveted appointment with her stylist to have her roots colored? He liked all the different hues and tones she'd had when they'd first met.

Forgetting about the fact that he'd nearly lost his leg and bled to death, their relationship had been based on superficial feelings and some pretty amazing sex. But absolutely no depth of feelings, no intimate sharing of goals and dreams, and most of all, no deep abiding faith or trust in one another.

In essence, everything he'd found within one short week after pulling a lovely woman from the depths of that lake.

Shaking his head, he knew Melanie needed to protect her pride by striking out at him and part of the reason he'd felt a flicker of relief when he'd found the ring on his kitchen table.

"Where is she?"

He looked over his shoulder and saw Dermot O'Halloran striding toward Michael's office. Instead of saying anything, he stepped aside. He'd wait until Bridget was feeling better before he talked to her again.

"Dermot?"

The weak voice belonged to the woman he'd promised to marry, the one who told him she loved him and she wanted to marry him.

But that was a few days ago, when he'd thought she was crazy. Now that he realized how lucky he'd been, he hoped it wasn't too late to fix the mess he'd made of things.

Forget about ghosts, leprechauns, and faeries. Bridget was the one who really mattered, not the threat of what those otherworldly creatures would do to himself or his cousins and their pub.

By the time he'd followed along behind Dermot, the big man was sitting on the sofa beside his sister. "But you don't understand," he heard her telling her brother. "Megan loves you."

"Then why was she wrapped around Tom Skinner?" Her brother's voice was suspiciously raspy.

Duncan wondered if this Megan had the ability to bring Dermot to his knees the way Bridget had brought Duncan to his.

"*He* was wrapped around *her.*"

"Well then," her brother said. "That's another matter entirely, isn't it, Sweeney?"

Michael agreed and looked up as Duncan walked into the room.

"There are times when it pays to listen to what a woman says," Michael said, trying not to smile.

Duncan wondered why. Then he saw that Bridget was staring at him, and the look in her eyes left absolutely no doubt in his mind that she cared.

"Bridget, I—"

"What do you want, Garvey?" O'Halloran demanded, getting in Duncan's face.

"To see if Bridget is all right."

"Haven't you done enough?" Dermot demanded, pushing Duncan backward.

He caught himself and pushed back. "No, I haven't, because for some reason your sister thought I would joke about asking someone to marry me."

"Hah!" Bridget said, rising to her feet.

"Then why didn't you answer me?" Duncan demanded.

"Because, you daft man." Bridget drilled her finger into the middle of his chest. "I didn't hear you."

"But you were looking right at me," he accused.

"And I was thinking about how you looked exactly like the reflection I saw in the lake when I fell in."

Duncan opened his mouth and then shut it. Twice.

"But I thought you wanted to—"

"Make you beg," she said, her words clipped, sharp as deadly weapons. "And so you've said."

"Well, I thought—"

"Wrong, it would seem," Michael said, coming over to where they stood.

"Just as you are about Megan," Bridget said to her brother.

Dermot frowned. "Maybe."

"Definitely," Megan said from where she stood in the doorway.

Dermot glared at her. "I saw what I saw."

The woman tilted her head to one side. "Even if you saw what you think you saw, doesn't what I feel in my heart for you count for anything?"

Duncan watched the big man's body react in shock to her words. Before he could fall over and hit the floor, Michael and Duncan had him eased back onto the couch.

"The bigger they are," Megan whispered to Bridget.

Bridget smiled at her friend. "And so it would seem."

Dermot recovered quickly enough and shoved to his feet. "Then you don't love Skinner?"

Megan started to speak but ended up shaking her head. "No you *eedjit*, I do not love Tom Skinner. How could I, when it's you I love?"

Dermot's goofy grin was a sight to behold. But not for too long. Duncan held out his hand to Bridget. "Will you listen now?"

Bridget took the hand he offered and slowly rose to stand beside him. "Yes," she whispered. "I'll listen."

Duncan brought her hand to his lips and pressed a kiss to the back of it, then turned it over and pressed another to the center of her palm.

Bridget swayed. He caught her against him and steadied her. When he was certain she wouldn't keel over, he got down on one knee. "Bridget O'Halloran," he began, his voice gaining strength as his love smiled at him. "Will you marry me?"

She looked at her brother and Megan and then at Michael before smiling at Duncan. "Why?"

"What kind of answer is that?"

"Easy now," a deep voice called out from the darkened corner of the room.

"Bollocks!"

"I've told ye to watch yer language around me Bridget."

Her eyes went round in wonder. "Great-grandda?" she whispered, "Is that really you?"

"Who else did you think would bring your young man up to scratch?" the ghost demanded, materializing at her side.

"I would have," her brother said. "If I thought he really wanted to marry her."

"We knew he did when he pulled her out of the lake," another voice said, joining the growing crowd in Michael's office.

"Seamus…" Duncan began.

"Will you look at that?" Megan rasped. "One of the gentry in the flesh!"

Dermot steadied Bridget with one arm and pulled her close.

"But 'twas the other night at Padraig's Ring that we knew for certain," a lilting voice drifted down from the ceiling.

And it was Dermot's turn to stare. "I'll be damned!"

"Lad, your language—" the ghostly O'Halloran began, only to be interrupted by the host of faeries that flew in to join the one hovering a few inches below the ceiling.

"We told ye to be careful what ye wished for, mortal," the tiny ebony-haired beauty reminded Bridget.

"That you did," Bridget agreed.

"Well then?" *Alainn Ceo* demanded.

"He's exactly what I wished for," Bridget said. "And the image I saw."

"Before ye got too greedy for another look and fell headfirst into the lake," her great-grandfather scolded.

"But Duncan was there to save me."

The ghost looked at the leprechaun, and the two in turn looked at the gathering group of faeries.

"That he was, lass," her great-grandfather answered. "That he was."

"Well then," Duncan said, clearing his throat. "You really did see faeries that day."

Bridget grinned at him. "I'm not entirely witless, you know."

Duncan looked at his cousin, who merely shrugged. Duncan finally said, "I know."

"Ye've yet to answer the man," the ghostly O'Halloran reminded her.

"I'm sorry," Bridget looked down at her feet. "If he'd just tell me why he wants to marry me, then maybe I might answer him."

Duncan drew her lips close to his and tasted the sweetness of her mouth. "Because you made me daft from the first moment I laid eyes on you."

"But I must have looked a sight, all drenched—"

"And so beautiful my heart aches whenever I think back to the day at the lake."

She blushed a becoming pink. "But what about Sean and my brother?"

"What about them?" Duncan demanded.

"Can you ever forgive them?"

Duncan looked at her brother and shrugged. "Does it matter that much to you?"

Tears filled her eyes. "Yes."

"I guess I can forgive them, then."

Bridget smiled through her tears. "You're a wonderful man, Duncan Garvey."

"I am, yes," he teased, lilting his words to mimic her soft brogue. "And lucky, too."

"Because?"

He grinned and lowered his head until their lips were a breath apart and only she would hear what he wanted to tell her. "Because we're going back to Padraig's Ring."

She turned a deeper shade of pink. "When?"

He lifted her in his arms. "How about now?"

The fluttering of tiny wings accompanied them on their way out of the pub's back door and all the way back to the ancient ring of stones.

As they stood within the ring of stones, the air shimmered and her great-grandfather appeared one last time. He pressed a kiss to Bridget's forehead, nodded to Duncan, and shook his hand.

As the moon's light dimmed, surrounded by a host of faeries, flanked by a ghost and a leprechaun, Duncan pledged his love to Bridget.

A rainbow rose up out of the mossy ground just inside the sacred ring of stones and arced above them.

"Duncan," she whispered. "Look!"

He shook his head, "Who'd believe me if I told them…rainbows and faeries…"

Bridget kissed his cheek. " 'Tis a blessing from the ancients."

Knowing fate had led him on this twisted, winding path to Bridget, Duncan pulled her close. "I'll love you forever Bridget O'Halloran."

"You were worth the wait and nearly drowning for," she whispered, lifting her lips for his tender kiss.

The rainbow shot sparks into the sky, the stones sang, the ground shook, and a ghostly figure smiled as he faded into the twilight. "Ah the beautiful children they'll make between them."

C.H. Admirand

Author's Note

Fate, destiny and love at first sight will always play a large part in my stories because they played a major role in my life. When I saw my husband for the first time, I knew he was the man I was going to spend the rest of my life with. I've loved him forever...well...more than half my life. Each and every hero I write about has a few of Dave's best qualities, his honesty, his integrity, his compassion for those in need and his killer broad shoulders. I'm such a sucker for a man with broad shoulders.

Catch up with the latest on my website at www.chadmirand.com .

I love to hear from readers! You can write to me at chadmirand@chadmirand.com or visit me on Facebook:
https://www.facebook.com/CHAdmirandBooks
or my blog
http://romanceauthor-chadmirand.blogspot.com/

Sláinte!
C.H. Admirand

Author's Bio

C.H. was born in Aiken, South Carolina, but her parents moved back to northern New Jersey where she grew up, which if you've met her would explain a lot. She's always had her nose in a book, has traveled the world over, and even tested the time-space continuum, thanks to the awesome power of the written word. One of her writing quirks is that she loves to include bits and pieces of her ancestors and ancestry in all of her books. Her family centers her and keeps her sane, which is why she enjoys adding elements of family, hearth, and home in all of her romances.

With 11 short stories and 15 novels to her credit, this award-winning, multi-published author's books are available in paperback, hardcover, trade paperback, magazine, e-book, large print, and audiobook.

Rainbow of Destiny

Proof

65776401R00133

Made in the USA
Charleston, SC
01 January 2017